FOREVER AND A DAY

A Novel

By

J.S. Smith

FOREVER AND A DAY
By J. S. Smith

PRESENT

It was a bluebird day; one of those sun-drenched, blue sky, see forever kind of days when just being alive seems reason enough.

Noah Johnson enjoyed the warmth of the sun, thankful for how good it felt on his arthritic joints. He had started out early on his walk, wanting to reach his destination before it became too hot, but it was farther than he remembered. Already he was perspiring and he still had a long way to go. When he was young, it seemed to take only minutes to move from the lake, following the stream up the mountain to the spot which had become his special place.

He continued around the lake where he loved to fish, through the meadow with its myriad of plants, and began trudging up the trail. He could feel the scrape of bone in his dried, arthritic, knee joints. His sweat converged into rivulets, running down his chest and soaking his shirt. He wanted to stop, but forced himself to continue, choosing to ignore the advice of his son, who was also his doctor. Both his son and daughter had admonished him for not slowing down and taking better care of himself. But he knew that after all these years, this might be the last time he would, or could, make the trip.

The pines and aspens were thinner now and he realized he was almost there.

"A few more steps," he thought. "Just a few more steps and I'll be there." He walked along the path, occasionally slipping on the loose gravel while concentrating on his feet, willing them to move up the increasingly steep trail. His breath became labored. Finally, he had to stop. He sucked in the moist morning air, looked up and there it was, his place, her place --- their place.

The granite outcropping stood before him, glistening as the morning sun played across its mica-flecked surface. It was like a monument to a distant memory, old as time. A silent sentinel belched from the very bowels of the earth. He took off his daypack and sat down at the rock's base. Opening the pack, he removed a bottle of water and took a long swallow then wet his bandana and wiped his sweat-streaked face. His shoulder was hurting and his left arm tingled. The necklace around his neck felt heavy and he reached up to rearrange it. He leaned back against the rock base that was still in shadow. He began to feel somewhat rejuvenated as he enjoyed its cool surface.

He looked across the vista before him and saw the trail he had just come up winding down to the valley below, then past it to the base of the mountain, the meadow he had just come up, the lake, the houses of which there were many more, and all newer than when he first saw them. Beyond that there were the surrounding mountains; eternal and yet ever changing.

"Thank you, Lord, for such a beautiful day and place," he said with a catch in his throat.

The effects of the walk and the warm morning sun were beginning to take their toll. He lowered his head to rest a moment. As he was looking down, a movement in the grass before him caught his eye. He saw an ant trying to move the carcass of a beetle. It stood among the blades of grass and was almost indistinguishable in the verdant, landscape. He studied it, intrigued by its efficiency; how it wasted no more energy than necessary. He watched as it struggled, marveling at its determination and will. He started to hum a few verses of the song "High Hopes," about an ant trying to move a rubber tree plant. The longer he studied the ant, the more his mind began to wander back to that other time so long ago. A thought came to him, something he had once heard someone say about how old men seemed to dream less and reminisce more. "How true," he thought, and smiled.

He leaned his head back and rested it against the coolness of the rock as his thoughts began to slip into the time streams of his memory. Back to the summer of his twentieth year, the summer he came to spend with his grandparents, the summer he had first known the pleasure and the pain of being truly alive.

CHAPTER 1
1939

"How much farther is it?" Noah asked. He knew exactly, but it was a game he had played with his father for as long as he could remember.

"About an hour," his father replied with a laugh. It was always 'about an hour.' Noah became anxious as he watched the surroundings change from the flat prairie land to the incline of the foothills that were the beginning of the mountains. He realized that just a few ridges away, after few more twists and turns, he would be in the mountains at the lake with his grandparents. It was the one place where he felt truly at home and alive.

He, his parents, his brother and the maid had been traveling all morning and he was tired, ready to enjoy the beginning of his summer in the same way he had for most of his life. Every year after school was out, his father would drive him, his fourteen-year-old brother, Michael, and his mother, to Fairview, where his grandparents lived. They would stay two weeks and then go back home, but this year, as a graduation present from college; they were leaving him behind for the summer. There, nestled in the mountains by the lake was the town of Fairview, where his heart resided and which, for the next few months, would be his home. He needed the time to figure out what he wanted to do now that he had graduated from college. It seemed to him that being surrounded by the idyllic setting of Fairview and the people he loved so much would make it easier to plan.

Normally it was hot and tiring confined in the car with the four of them, traveling the eight or so hours. But this year it was even worse since his mother had insisted they bring their colored housekeeper, Thelma, with them. She had come to work for his family when he was in grade school and he realized that she had been about his age now when she started. It was a good thing that she was just a wisp of a woman since Noah, Michael, and Thelma had to share the back seat, making the heat even more noticeable in the cramped space. Noah didn't mind, since Thelma had in many ways been more of a mother and confidante to both his brother and him than their own mother had been. Once when he was five, he had thrown flour on Thelma in an attempt to make her white. He had received a spanking from his mother for his efforts and an admonishment that "God did not want her white". It had been Thelma who took care of his brother and him when his mother was away at club meetings. It was Thelma who fed them, did their laundry, and made them clean their rooms. He had spent many hours sitting in the kitchen talking to her while she prepared their meals. In truth, Noah enjoyed her company more than he enjoyed that of his mother's.

"Mom, I'm hot," whined Michael. They had left when it was still dark, but now that the sun had been up for several hours the temperature was rising. At the reminder, Noah reached up and wiped off the beads of sweat which had formed on his forehead and lip.

"I know Michael," his mother replied. "I'm hot too." As if to reinforce her statement, she took a washrag from her purse, wetting it with ice water from a thermos. "Here," she said, handing him the damp rag. "Wash your face with this."

Arthur Johnson looked at his wife. "Louise, can't we roll down the windows a little more?"

"Arthur," she replied, "the wind blows in too much dirt, and besides, it isn't good for the boys." Noah wanted to say he didn't mind the wind, but he knew it would be useless to say so.

"Anyway," she continued, "we're about there."

Noah knew this was true and decided it was better to just sit back and endure the remaining few minutes. His mother always seemed to get her way. Noah's thoughts drifted back to the time she had insisted they drive a hundred miles out of their way to see an ancient lava flow, only to discover that the highway now ran through it. She had insisted it would be, "good for the boys to see." By the time they arrived, it was dark and since the lava beds were black they saw nothing!

He listened to the thump of the tires on the road's expansion joints and watched the small, rubber-bladed fan as it oscillated on the dash, making more noise than moving air. He felt that at twenty years old he could endure anything, even an eight-hour trip in a cramped '37 Chevrolet with the windows rolled up; if the end would bring him back to the place he truly loved. He pictured in his mind the small town nestled in the valley surrounded by the mountains. He could see the lake with its azure blue, cold, water even in the summer, where his grandfather had taught him to fish. He still remembered catching his first fish when he was five, and how proud he had felt. His grandfather had made him feel as if he had caught some wary leviathan that, until then, had lingered safely in the depths. He remembered, too, how his mother, rather than making over it, had told him to take it outside before it smelled up the house.

Noah looked out the window and noticed the trees had changed from the stockier oaks, cedar, mesquite, and scrubs, to the loftier conifers, laurels, and aspens. He forgot the stuffy confines of the car as the beauty and excitement of the surroundings took effect, along with the smell and feel of the drier, cleaner, cooler, air.

His father rolled his window down, pushed out the wing glass and said, "Smell that air. We don't have to worry about dirt now. Besides its much cooler."

"All right, Arthur," replied his mother with some chagrin. "If we all become sick, I won't be to blame."

"God, not another argument," Noah thought. It seemed lately that was all they did. He recognized the area they were passing through. "Just one more hill," he thought, staring ahead in anticipation. Suddenly there it was. Noah stared down at the valley and the lake it contained. He could make out several of the houses and businesses that made up the town of Fairview and he felt energized.

He knew he would soon see his grandparents, whom he adored, and his friend Sam, a colored man who worked as a handyman and made woodcarvings of animals to sell to the tourists. Noah's grandfather was a doctor, but his passion was fishing and tying flies that he sold in Joseph Hartley's general store; the money they made went to help support the small clinic he operated. His grandfather was more than Noah's friend, he was his mentor, and would take time to show Noah the world that surrounded him at the lake. He had a way with words and always seemed to say the right thing at the right time. He had taught Noah how to fish for the trout that were in the lake and streams. Everyone knew that George Johnson was not just the valley's only doctor but its best fisherman as well. In truth, he taught Noah everything he knew about life and Noah worshipped him.

"I see nothing has changed," his mother said disdainfully, as they passed Joseph Hartley's general store.

"Nope," his father answered, "and I like the comfort in that." Noah looked at his father, trying to imagine him being a boy growing up here. He had a hard time visualizing that since his father was not a large man and did not possess the kind of strong, rugged, backwoods feature that was the stereotype of those who grew up in the mountains. His unimposing stature, along with the graying hair and bald spot, gave him a rather dowdy appearance.

His father had left after high school to attend college and, except for short visits, never returned. He spent most of his time at the grocery store he owned back home. Noah's mother, on the other hand, had grown up in the city and never seemed quite at ease here at the lake. She had the smooth, pampered skin that came from a lack of exposure to sun and wind. Her peroxide blond hair was a stylish coiffure to mimic the movie star Veronica Lake and her clothes were of the latest fashion. She, along with his father and brother, would stay two weeks and she would make a pretense of enjoying herself.

Noah knew it was a facade since he had seen the bottles of Lysol she carried with her and used whenever they stopped to use the restroom or to eat. She even used it at his grandparents. He knew she missed the city, the clubs, the shops, the restaurants, the cleaners, the services, and the movies. It was the main reason she insisted on bringing the maid Thelma with them on this trip, even though his father had protested. "You don't need her," he had said. "Mother can do just fine. Besides, I think she'll resent her."

"Nonsense," his mother had replied. "Your mother will enjoy not having to wait on us hand and foot. She'll enjoy herself so much more, and it will make it much easier for her to take care of Noah after we leave."

Noah was glad that Thelma would be there but resented the fact that his father gave in rather than stand up to his mother. He had often wondered if she made his father sit down to pee. One event on the trip had troubled Noah. His mother had insisted they stop at a certain roadside diner for lunch, one that was recommended by Duncan Hines. When they got out, Noah had asked Thelma if she was going to join them. She looked flustered and mumbled something about just waiting in the car and maybe they could bring her something. Noah noticed his mother looked chagrined and his father looked away. At first Noah didn't understand, and then he saw the sign—

NO COLOREDS

"Oh," he said and went in, but it still bothered him.

Noah's thoughts were interrupted when his father announced, "We're here!" Noah loved the cabin where his grandparents lived. It had a front porch that ran the length of the house and a high green gabled roof. There was a small clinic connected by a breezeway on one side. His grandfather had cut most of the logs himself when he arrived fresh from medical school to become the first doctor in the valley. All the neighbors pitched in to help with building and George and Mary moved in within two weeks. Noah loved the log home, with its chinked walls, stone fireplace, and exposed beam ceilings. He thought it was the epitome of a "cabin in the woods." They had recently added an indoor bathroom since President Roosevelt and the W.P.A. had brought electricity and water to the valley. They had even acquired telephone service that caused several of the locals to complain it was getting too "citified."

They drove past the general store/grocery, the drugstore/ice cream parlor, several churches, the one room school house and a few homes.

As his father stopped the car, Noah jumped out. He ran up the steps and onto the porch. Just as he started to knock, the door flew open and there stood his grandparents.

"Granddad!" he said, and even though at twenty he considered himself a man in control of his emotions, he couldn't help throwing his arms around the old man and hugging him. Then he turned to his grandmother and hugged and kissed her.

"Noah," his father called. "Come back here and help me with the luggage."

"Yes sir," Noah answered, although in truth he longed to change into his jeans and hiking boots and begin the exploration of his surroundings. It was here he could lose himself and become fully alive. He rushed back to the car and began to gather up the luggage. "You can help too, Michael," he said to his brother, who scowled back at him.

As Noah started to the house, he noticed his grandmother looking uncertainly at Thelma, who in turn was hesitantly moving forward.

"Mary," Noah's mother said, "this is Thelma, our housekeeper." She waited, and when she saw the incredulous look on her mother-in-law's face, she continued. "I thought it would be so much easier for you if we brought her along to help."

"My dear," his grandmother answered, "having you all here is never a problem." Noah detected a slight change in her voice. "I always enjoy having you here and being able to make over you." Then she looked at Thelma. "What's done is done and you're welcome here Thelma. We have plenty of room and I'm sure you'll be a big help. Come on in and let's get settled."

It was decided that Noah and Michael would share a room and Thelma would sleep on a cot in the wash room.

"How was the trip, son?" his grandfather asked his father.

"Long and hot," was his reply.

His father turned to Noah and Michael. "Let's get that luggage inside."

"Let me give you a hand," his grandfather said to Noah. "I'm anxious to show you some new flies I tied. I'm taking a couple of weeks off from the clinic, unless there is an emergency. That way we will be able to spend some time together."

"I'm home," Noah said to himself with a smile.

CHAPTER 2

"The sun feels good," Noah thought. He had hurried through the chores his father had given him, visited with his grandfather, who insisted he look over the new flies he had tied, and then rushed to change clothes. This was what he had been waiting for; anticipating the hike to his favorite place - a rock outcropping high up on the face of the mountain. The granite monolith was in a small clearing by a stream, at the edge of the timberline. He loved to climb over it or just lean against it, relishing in the coolness of the granite.

From this spot, he could see down the mountain to the bowl-shaped valley and the lake with the town at the far end. The mountains surrounding the valley had rocky spires that seemed to touch heaven. To him, it was the most beautiful sight in the world and one where he could sit and enjoy the splendor for hours. When Noah was younger, he would come to this place and pretend that he was a king and everything below him was his kingdom. Now that he was older, he simply enjoyed the view. If he sat quietly he would often see deer, marmots, and chipmunks and, although he had never seen them, he knew elk, bear and even an occasional mountain lion lived in the area.

Noah was physically uninspiring with a tall, willowy frame that gave him a rather awkward appearance. His brother, Michael, on the other hand, was physically endowed, an extrovert who enjoyed people, parties, sports and action. In contrast, Noah preferred to be alone or with a few, close, mostly older friends. He never associated with or felt comfortable around kids his own age. The only exception was David Lewis, a neighbor boy with whom he shared a commonality even though David played football and dated a number of girls. They had gone to the same schools and even graduated from the same high school. David had gone to work after graduation while Noah went on to finish college, graduating in three years. Now he was trying to decide what he wanted to do. His father suggested he might like to work in the grocery store, but he was not certain that was for him. This trip was partly to give him time to think about his future. He loved his family but he knew that even though it had provided a good living for the family he could not follow his father into a career of managing the store.

It had been a long climb, but one he thoroughly enjoyed. He loved the beauty of the meadow with its myriad colors and sweet, spicy, floral smells. He equally loved the woods with their dappled, filtered hues and damp, earthy smell. He had not acclimated to the altitude and had to stop occasionally to rest. He finally reached his spot and stood looking out at the valley, then sat down, resting against the rock, enjoying the feel of the cool stone on his sweaty back. He looked up and saw a hawk carrying a small rodent in its talons. He watched as it alternately flew to gain altitude, and then glide, the weight of its prey pulling it down. The hawk tried to stay aloft, not wanting to expend more energy than its meal would bring. Noah liked being out in nature where everything seemed so ordered and made such sense. He wished that over the years of his childhood, his father had been more inclined to enjoy nature with him. Noah was grateful that his father provided a good living for his family, but still there seemed a void; one that his grandfather filled.

Noah began to relax, letting his thoughts wander, when suddenly he heard a rustling in the bushes by the trail. His heart began to pound. He thought it might be a bear since it was making too much noise to be a deer; then he remembered his grandfather had told him that black bear would avoid you if they knew you were there. He tried to shout but it only came out as a croak. He swallowed, and tried again. Just as he managed to produce a small yelp a large black dog came into the clearing and began to bark.

He looked incredulously at the dog and then laughed. "Hey boy," he called. The dog took a few steps forward, wagging his tail and barking.

"What are you doing here?" Noah asked. "Come on, come here." The dog barked again and came to him.

"Good boy," Noah said, running his hands over the dog's back, "Who do you belong to?"

"Me," a female voice replied.

Noah looked up, startled. "Oh," was all he could say.

"Actually, he's my uncle's." She said

Noah was mesmerized by her looks and found himself staring at her as she stood in the clearing. Her eyes were incredible; large, dark, and deep. The sunlight filtering through the trees made her ink black hair shine and highlighted the sprinkling of freckles across her nose. She was wearing a yellow sundress that was shimmering on her tall and willowy frame. Positioned as she was in both sun and shadow, she took on an ethereal look.

"Oh," Noah repeated. "He's friendly."

"Yes, he's a good dog" she replied, rubbing behind the dog's ears. "His name is Beau, after Beau Brummell, like in the movie."

Noah smiled, "Well, he is rather dapper looking." He said.

"I'm Ann." She said smiling.

"Ann," He repeated, letting it linger for a moment before replying, "I'm Noah."

"Noah, that's a strange name - - but pretty". She said.

"It's biblical. You know, Noah and the flood?" He said.

"Yes, I know." She said.

"Do you live around here?" He asked.

"No, no, I'm from France, from Paris." she replied.

"I thought you had kind of an accent". He said.

"I've been in America before, and I've studied English for a long time," she replied, with what seemed to Noah to be a note of defensiveness. She turned and looked out over the scene below. "It's pretty up here." She said as if she was in awe with the scene before her.

"Yeah, it's my favorite place." He said.

"I can see why. Now it's mine too. Mind if I sit down?" She came over and sat down next to him, reaching over to rub Beau's head. "It's so peaceful up here," she said. "It's like nothing can touch you."

"Yeah, I know. I used to come here and pretend I was the king and that was my kingdom below." He said with a sweep of his hands.

She laughed, "King Noah." She reached down and picked up a stick. "Here is your scepter, my lord." She said with a bow.

Noah took it, feeling a little foolish.

"Thanks. I will reign over all around me." Noah said with a wave of his hand.

"Can I be queen?" she asked, amused.

"Sure." Noah answered. He looked at her and thought she was the most beautiful girl he had ever seen. He loved how her black hair hung down, glistening in the sunlight. And then there were her eyes. Her eyes were incredible. They seemed to suck him into her. He remembered reading somewhere about eyes being the window of the soul, and in her case he had to agree.

"You said you're from France?" Noah asked.

"Yes, from Paris, the 'City of Light'," she replied. "I came over to spend the summer with my uncle and aunt. Their name is Zimmerman. Do you know them?" She asked.

"No," he answered, "but I don't live here either", he added. "I'm like you, just visiting for the summer. I'm staying with my grandfather, George Johnson, you know, the doctor, and my grandmother Mary. I visit them every summer, usually for a few weeks, but this time I'm staying all summer. It's a graduation present from college." Noah added.

"Me too, except in my case its graduation from what you call high school." Ann leaned her head back and closed her eyes. Suddenly she sat upright and turned towards him.

"Do you think there will be a war?" she asked.

Noah was taken aback. It was something that the adults talked about a lot. Even among his peers it was discussed, but he hadn't thought much about it.

"I don't know," he said shrugging his shoulders, "Maybe." He said pensively.

"I think there will be one," she continued. "I'm afraid," she added, giving an uncontrollable shiver.

Noah noticed her whole demeanor had changed. She suddenly seemed sad.

"Oh well," she said, appearing to recover. "It's too pretty a day. Let's not talk about it." She waved her hand in a sweeping gesture. "Besides this is your kingdom, King Noah, and we're perfectly safe." She raised her arm to brush away an insect and noticed Noah staring at her. "Is something wrong?" she asked.

"No, no I just ---," Noah said hesitantly, feeling his face reddening, "I have always heard French women don't shave under their arms." He said.

She was momentarily caught by surprise and then laughed, "I think you have the French mixed up with the Italians." She said.

Noah looked sheepishly, "I'm sorry." He said, humbly.

"It's okay. Actually, they don't shave in the country, but I live in Paris and we are humbly modern. "'Tres chic'," she said by way of explanation.

Noah found himself glancing at her, not wanting to be seen. She turned suddenly, catching him and stared back for a moment, and then smiled. Noah was at first disconcerted, then relaxed, finding solace in her smile.

"You know I really envy you for the beauty and sereneness of this place." She said, waving her hand in an ark.

"Yeah I always look forward to being here." He exclaimed, then looking thoughtful for a moment added, "So tell me what's life like in Paris?"

"It's so lovely. There is so much music, art, beauty and life going on every day," she answered.

"What about your parents?" Noah asked.

"My father is in banking and finance and my mother is involved in social activities and homemaking. My younger sister Rachael, is in school., we are four years apart in age. She said, then asked, "What about your family?"

"My father is from here in Fairview," then added, "but he couldn't wait to get away. He left right after high school and moved to the Dallas area where we live today. He started a grocery store at home and spends most of his time there. My mom, like yours, is into home, club work, and socializing. My brother, Michael is fourteen and nothing like me. He is into athletics and works part time in my father's store. He is like my father and doesn't like the mountains."

They talked a little longer, until Ann said she needed to start home. She got up to go, "I enjoyed meeting you, your 'Majesty''. She smiled and bowed in gesture eliciting a laugh from Noah.

"Yeah, me too you," he said, then reached down and rubbed Beaus head. "You too Beau." He added.

"Come on Beau," she said, and started walking toward the shade where the tree line began.

"Wait a minute I'll walk back with you." Noah said, getting up and moving to her. Just before they walked into the shadows he turned and looked back at the rock. He had the strange feeling that it had grown significantly in the fabric of his life.

CHAPTER 3

Noah could not concentrate on anything but Ann. No matter how he tried, his thoughts came back to her; to the place where they had met. He could still see her standing at the edge of the timberline between shadow and sun. Her image took on a mystical appearance as it shimmered in the reflected heat. He knew he would never forget that sight

He had not been home for long before his grandfather noticed a change in him.

"Something bothering you Noah?" his grandfather asked.

"No, Sir," Noah answered.

His Grandfather stared at him. "Come on Noah, I know something's bothering you. Are you sick?"

"No, I guess I - - I'm just thinking about someone I met today." He said.

"Oh," his grandfather answered with a smile. "Who is she?"

Noah was surprised by his grandfather's perception, then answered, "Her name's Ann."

"What's her last name?" asked his grandfather.

"Meyer. She's visiting from France, from Paris," Noah volunteered. "She's staying with her uncle, Mr. Zimmerman." Noah said.

"Ira Zimmerman? I think his wife's name is Ruth. He runs the drugstore. Bought it not long after Sid Thomas died; he bought Sid's house too. They're Jewish, aren't they?" asked his grandfather.

"I don't know," said Noah, surprised by the question.

"Well, I'm sure she's a nice girl," said his grandfather. He changed the subject and asked, "How would you like to go fishing in the morning?" He asked enthusiastically.

"I'd love it," answered Noah, then suddenly added, "May I ask Ann?"

His grandfather hesitated then said, "Sure, if it's okay with the Zimmerman's. We'll leave around seven." He said.

"Okay. Thanks Grandpa, I'll let Ann know." Then he added, "I think you will like her." Noah said.

"I'm sure I will. Go call her and then we can eat," said his grandfather.

Noah went into the hall, picked up the phone and asked the operator if she could connect him to the Zimmerman's.

"Hello?" A male voice answered.

"Mr. Zimmerman? May I speak to Ann?"

"Who is this?" came the reply.

"This is Noah Johnson, Doctor Johnson's grandson. I'm staying with Dr. Johnson and my grandmother for the summer. I met your niece today." He said trying to sound matter of fact even though he could feel his heart beating faster and took a deep breath.

"Just a minute." There was a long pause and Noah could hear conversation in the background. After what seemed an eternity Ann answered.

"Hello Noah. "She said cheerfully.

Noah tried not to sound nervous. "Hi Ann. I was just wondering if you would like to go fishing with my grandfather and me tomorrow. We'll leave around seven in the morning. We need to get an early start. The fish don't bite well when it warms up. We have everything you'll need so you won't need to bring a thing." He realized he was rambling and stopped.

"I would love to. Let me ask." she replied.

There was another pause and again he could hear conversation. This time he could make out Ann's pleading voice. Finally, she returned.

"I can go. Are you sure I don't need to bring anything? What do I wear?" She asked.

Noah almost dropped the receiver in his excitement. "Nothing", then he laughed, " I mean there's nothing you need to bring." He could hear her laughing. "Just wear jeans and a long-sleeved shirt in case the mosquitoes are bad. You'll need a hat with a brim to keep the sun off. We'll meet you in the morning at your house around seven."

"Noah, would it be all right if I bring Beau?" She asked.

"Sure," Noah answered, certain his grandfather wouldn't mind. "Thank you, God," he whispered. He hung up the phone and leaned against the wall until he calmed down.

Noah sat down at the table with the rest of his family. When Thelma brought out the food from the kitchen, Noah noticed his grandmother seemed nervous. "I feel silly having someone waiting on me," she said.

"Nonsense, that's why we brought Thelma along. You deserve a rest," his mother replied, patting her mother-in-law's arm.

"Noah and I are going fishing in the morning," his grandfather announced, wanting to change the subject.

Noah was relieved that his grandfather had not mentioned taking Ann. He did not want to answer all the questions he knew his mother would ask.

"Well," said his father, "looks like you picked a good day for it."

He was hungry. He had been hunting on the other side of the mountain at the far end of his territory. The small, furry, animals that lived in the meadow below had been easy prey until one evening, when one of the two-legged, funny smelling animals had suddenly appeared with a thunder stick. There had been a sharp pain in his hip as he turned to run. He instinctively went to the spot where the water coming from the rock made a mud hole. There, he wallowed and rolled in the soothing wet earth, making sure to coat the area where the hurt was. He rested for several days until he could walk, but he still had pain and now he felt hot and thirsty. He knew he must eat to maintain his strength, but he had lost some of his natural agility. He had a hard time catching mice, chipmunks and rabbits that he usually caught with ease; deer were impossible. He could smell and hear the sounds coming from the two-legged animal's lair below, at the bottom of the mountain. He normally would not approach such a place, but he was hungry, weak and desperate.

He walked slowly through the brush until he was near the two-legged one's den. He could not see or smell it, but he remained cautious. He saw the feathered creatures and the one small, horned animal and his stomach ached even more. Cautiously, he eased forward, when suddenly a barker animal ran towards him. It came at him and the noise it made hurt his hot head. He bared his teeth and let out a screech. The barking one hesitated, and then continued at him. He unsheathed his claws and took a swipe with his powerful forepaw. It raked across the flank of the barking one and it whimpered and retreated.

The effort and excitement had made him feel even weaker and more in pain. He turned and skulked off, but he knew he would not, could not, give up.

Noah was suffering from having had a hard time thinking of Ann and the upcoming morning. They were to get an early start the next morning. Noah's grandmother packed them a lunch and Noah ate a bowl of oatmeal while his grandfather ate his toast and coffee. After finishing they set out to meet Ann. When they approached the Zimmerman house, she and Beau came out. She was carrying a sack of cookies that her aunt had made. Ann's long black hair was in braids and an old floppy hat was perched on her head. The effect of the hat, along with the faded flannel shirt and worn jeans on her willowy frame, gave her the look of a scarecrow. But even then, Noah thought she was the most beautiful girl he had ever seen. He was so proud to have her with him and his grandfather. Beau seemed to enjoy seeing Noah again. He licked Noah's hand as he reached out to pet him. Noah introduced Ann and Beau to his grandfather and they started around the lake for the stream that lay at its far end.

Noah loved this early time of day when the ground was covered with dew and mist rose off of the lake. They walked for almost an hour, munching on the cookies whenever they stopped to rest. Finally, they arrived at the convergence of the stream and the lake.

"On up the creek about a quarter mile is a good hole," George said. "We can probably catch some nice ones there."

They worked their way up the stream, being careful not to slip on the wet and moss-covered rocks. Hundreds of mosquitoes swarmed around them from every direction, each one possessed with some primordial instinct to eat its fill before it mated and died.

"See," Noah said to Ann, grunting between slaps. "Now you know why I suggested you wear a long sleeve shirt and pants. They will disperse as the sun warms things up. "

They reached a spot where the quick water and green, slippery, moss- covered rocks gave way to a quiet pool of darker colored water that was about thirty feet across. Noah was enthralled with the incredible clean smell of the air infused with the damp earth, wildflowers, and balsam.

"Try not to move around too much," said George. "Trout are easily spooked."

They eased up to the pool and Ann gave Beau the last cookie telling him to sit, then they began to prepare their lines. George took out his pipe and filled it with Prince Albert tobacco from the can. When he lit it and the smoke rose up around him, Noah thought that, with his white beard and the wreath of smoke, he looked a little like Santa Claus. The thought reminded him of the story his family told about when his grandmother had made his grandfather a Santa suit to wear to a Christmas party where he would hand out candy and presents to all the kids in Fairview. The only problem was that since he was the only doctor in the valley, he had treated all of the children in his office and they all knew his voice. When he made his entrance as Santa with his ho, ho, ho's, every child over two had said, "That's not Santa Claus, that's Dr. George". He never again tried to play Santa, and his grandmother cut up the suit and used the fabric in one of her quilts.

Noah marveled at the dexterity his grandfather displayed with his gnarled, arthritic hands as he tied onto the tippet what looked like a piece of fuzz.

"Here, Ann," George said handing the rod to her. "Let me show you how to cast this thing."

He explained how the secret was to let the weight of the line create momentum to carry the fly thirty feet or so.

"It's like a clock," he explained. "Think of your head as being 12 o'clock, and then you move the rod between 10 and 1 o'clock on the dial." He showed her with his rod, and then let her try.

Noah watched fascinated, as the two of them worked together. He remembered the first time he had gone fishing with his grandfather. He had been around five and George had given him a fishing pole with a piece of cheese attached to the hook for bait. Noah had ended up catching a brookie that was about six inches long but anyone listening to him would have thought it was some rare aquatic beast. To this very day he kept the memory of that time in his heart.

On her first try Ann brought the rod too far back, causing the line to miss Beau by only a few inches. Beau barked and prudently moved back out of the way.

"Sorry Beau," Ann laughed.

Noah had his line ready and began to cast. Everything came back to him quickly, as he felt the rhythm of the cast return. After several casts he suddenly had a strike. He set the hook and pulled in a nice, eight-inch brook trout.

"Nice going," George said. He was still working with Ann. "Put it in the creel. Don't forget to gut it first," he added.

Noah prepared the fish and then placed it, along with several handfuls of wet vegetation, inside the old willow creel his grandfather always carried. He noticed Ann was now beginning to cast with more proficiency. He watched her for a moment then went back and began to fish again. After a few more casts he caught another brookie, and as the morning wore on, he caught several more.

All of a sudden both Ann and his grandfather gave out a loud whoop.

"Keep the rod tip high," shouted George. "Fight him with the rod. Don't let the line go slack." Suddenly the fish broke the surface and for a second was suspended in the air. "That's no brookie," George said, excitedly. "That's a Brown!" The fish was about eighteen inches long. It was a darker, greenish- brown that glistened in the morning sunlight. "That a girl," said George. "Keep the line tight. We don't want to lose it. Noah get the net ready." He said enthusiastically.

Noah moved quickly to pick up the net. Ann, with George's help, managed to work the fish to the shore and Noah stepped out carefully onto a moss-covered rock to scoop it up.

"Careful now," George said. Just as he managed to coax it into the net, Noah lost his footing and fell, seat first, into the shallow water. As he landed he lost his grip on the net and it went flying, along with the fish, onto the bank. The fish disgorged the hook and began flopping towards the water. His grandfather wasn't fast enough, and Ann couldn't hold on to the slick fish. Just as it was about to escape into the water Beau pounced upon it, penning it with his paws.

"Good boy," said George as he reached down and managed to secure the fish through the gills. "Noah, you okay?" he asked.

"Yes," Noah answered in a dejected voice as he managed to get up.

"Well, I think we've had enough excitement for one morning," said George. He turned to Noah. "Sorry we don't have any dry clothes. You sure you're okay?" Noah nodded in affirmation. "Let's get this fish taken care of and eat our lunch." He held up the trout. "That's some fish. You did really well Ann." He reached down and patted Beau. "So, did you Beau. So, did you."

After they ate the sandwiches and fruit they had brought, they began the journey home. Noah looked at Ann and had a vague thought that he had met someone who, in only two days' time, made him feel as if they had shared a lifetime of experiences. He no longer seemed to notice the wet, cold, clamminess of his jeans.

CHAPTER 4

After much debate with his mother who did not like home caught fish, she only liked ones served in restaurants, it was decided to have the ones they caught for dinner. George gave them to Mary to cook and, over her objections, Louise had insisted that Thelma help. Noah told his mother that he wanted to invite a friend, Ann. His mother hesitated; not knowing who Ann was until George explained that Ann had accompanied them and related the story of how Ann and her dog Beau had caught the largest fish. Finally, to Noah's great relief, his mother gave in and began to plan, as she put it, "A grand feast."

Thelma showed Mary her "special" seasoning for fish, a combination of cornmeal, flour, and spices, which after some reluctance, Mary admitted tasted wonderful.

"The real secret," Thelma told her," is to have the oil real hot so that it will cook quickly and not absorb the grease." Thelma had also made her hot water cornbread that was one of Noah's favorites.

When Ann arrived, Noah introduced her to everyone. The only member of the morning's expedition not present was Beau. Louise had put her foot down and refused to acquiesce. "I'm not going to allow any dog into the house," she said. Noah knew she meant it. She thought that dogs and cats were dirty and carried disease. It was the main reason he had never had a dog. Even without Beau, Noah was happy that Ann was there.

"You certainly have a nice home Mrs. Johnson," Ann remarked as they sat down at the table.

"Thank you dear. It holds a lot of wonderful memories," Mary said, as Thelma brought out the food.

Mary was warming to Thelma's presence. She enjoyed sharing the cooking and trading recipes, something that never would occur between her and Louise. The truth was Louise had no interest in kitchen activities and was proud of herself for the smart decision she had made to bring Thelma. The smell of fried fish and onion-laced hot water cornbread permeated the dining room.

George gave a prayer thanking The Lord for this day, the food, and their new found friend, Ann.

The food tasted every bit as good as it looked and smelled. As they ate, George relived the day's adventure. He took great pains in relating it with embellishments allowed in fish tales, of Ann catching the big brown.

"Looks like you had more than beginner's luck," Arthur said to Ann. "You must be a natural."

"I've never fished before. It was fun." Ann replied.

"Your uncle's never taken you?" Arthur asked.

"No sir. There was no place to go before he moved here and now he's always busy working at the drugstore." Ann replied.

"What about your family?" Louise asked.

"None of them ever fished." Ann answered.

"No, I mean tell us about your family," Louise said, perturbed.

"We live in Paris. My father's a banker and my mother's a housewife. I have a younger sister, Rachel, who is in school. I've lived there all my life and have a lot of friends and relatives in the area. I just finished school and plan on going to the University." Ann said.

"What do you want to study?" Arthur asked.

"I was going to study music or art. I play the piano and also paint. I wanted to bring beauty into the world, but with everything that's happening, I don't know," Ann said

"Now more than ever, the world needs that beauty, so don't change your mind," George said, smiling.

Thelma came in bringing her famous bread pudding and everyone, except Louise, raved about the meal. She was becoming bored with the conversation.

"You're Jewish, aren't you?" Louise asked abruptly.

"Yes ma'am," Ann answered.
Noah noticed an air of disdain in her voice and decided it was time to change the subject. "Dad, Ann thinks there will be a war."

"Well, I think it is very possible. Hopefully diplomacy will prevail. These are very uncertain times we live in," Arthur said.

"I didn't like the Germans in the last war, and I certainly wouldn't trust that strutting, blowhard, Hitler," said George. He had been too old to serve in the last war but had endured many days trying to tend to the injured and to victims of the 1918 flu epidemic. "What do your parents think?" George asked Ann.

"They don't talk about it around my sister or me very much, but I think they are very worried," Ann looked at them with a solemn expression.

"Did you hear about 'Crystal Night'?" she continued.

"No, I don't think so," Arthur answered. The rest shook their heads no.

"Back in November, a group of Nazis went on a rampage in Berlin, killing Jews at random. They burned the largest synagogue and destroyed hundreds of other homes and places of worship. They called it 'Crystal Night' because of all the broken glass left after they destroyed the windows on Jewish businesses. They used it as an excuse, the assassination of a German diplomat by a young Jewish boy I knew in Paris. He said he was avenging the mistreatment of his parents in Germany. He told the authorities that, 'Being a Jew is not a crime. I am not a dog. The Jewish people have a right to live on the earth.'" She stopped and wiped away a tear, then took a deep breath in an attempt at regaining composure. "He said that anywhere he went he's been chased like an animal." Ann looked around at them and then began to cry. Mary got up and put her arms around her. "There, there, honey. It's okay," Mary said.

"I'm sorry," Ann said.

"Can we talk about something more pleasant?" Louise interjected. "I read that they are developing some kind of fabric that is like an artificial silk. They can make stockings out of it. I don't know what they'll think of next. I sure would like to go to the New York World's Fair. You know they are calling it 'The World of Tomorrow.'"

George looked at her and shook his head. "I'm afraid the 'World of Tomorrow' is going to be a pretty unpleasant place." George excused himself and went out on the porch to smoke his pipe.

Noah announced he and Ann were going for a walk.

"Stay near," Louise said.

Noah needed to go to the bathroom and asked Ann to wait for him on the porch. As he came out of the bathroom he overheard the conversation coming from the dining room.

"I don't know that I like him being with that girl," his mother said.

"Now Louise, she seems perfectly all right," said his father.

"She's from Paris, and besides, she's Jewish." Louise said with a note 0f disdain.

"She seems very sweet," Mary said. "And she's certainly pretty."

"Yeah," echoed Michael. He then began to tell them about his first day at the summer camp several of the local churches ran.

Ann had stepped out on the porch and spotted George sitting in a rocker, smoking his pipe. "Beautiful night," he said.

"Yes, it certainly is," She said. "Doctor Johnson can --"

"George," he corrected. "Fishing buddies don't need to be so formal."

"George, can I ask you something?"

"Of course, Honey," he said.

"Why does everyone hate the Jews?" She asked.

He was momentarily startled, not expecting such a serious and complex question. "don't know, but I don't think everyone hates or fears Jewish people. I know I don't. Part of it may be because they work hard and value success, which creates a lot of envy. Then too, we don't understand their culture, and human nature is to always distrust and fear what we don't understand. Humanity is always looking for a scapegoat to blame our own inadequacies on," he paused, studying her for a moment.

"I hope I helped."

"Thanks, you have." She said.

Noah walked onto the porch. "You ready?" he asked Ann.

"Yes," she answered. "Goodnight George."

"Well you have certainly become friends." Noah said as they walked away.

"He said I'm his fishing buddie." Ann said with a laugh.

"Goodnight you two. Enjoy the evening," George called out as they walked away.

It was one of those perfect mountain nights when the sky is luminous and the air is cool and dry. They walked past Hartley's General Store to the lake. At the lake they walked onto the pier and sat down on one of the wooden benches that lined it. They sat in silence for a while, listening to the sounds of the cicadas and frogs flowing across the summer night. Then Ann reached over and took Noah's hand. He could feel the warmth of her and it gave him a funny, hot, flushed, feeling.

"I like your family, especially your Grandfather." Ann said.

"Yeah, he's my favorite," Noah replied. "He talks a lot but what he says makes sense. He's the kindest man, and in his own way, the most intelligent person I've ever known."

"I really enjoyed today." Ann said. "Noah, I know this sounds crazy. We've only known each other two days but I feel like I've known you and this place forever."

"Me too," he said.

She turned and studied him. "What do you want to do now that you've finished college?"

"I don't know," he replied. "Go to work, I guess. My father wants me to help in the grocery store."

"Is that what you want?" she asked.

"I guess so," he looked at her, studying her. "No," he said, "No, I want to do something with my life. As much as I love him, I just cannot see myself following in his footsteps." That's one reason I wanted to spend the summer here, to try and figure my future course out without my parent's interference.

"I know you will find an answer." She said.

"What about you? What do you want to do?" he asked.

"Survive," she said.

"What do you mean?" he said, taken aback.

"Noah, it's easy for you. You're safe here in the mountains, in America. But I live in Europe, in France, and any minute we'll be in a war. Besides that, I'm Jewish." She said.

He looked at her quizzically.

"Does it bother you that I'm Jewish?" she asked.

He was caught off guard. "No," he said hesitantly, "I never even thought about it."

"It seemed to bother your mother." She said.

"Yeah, probably, but a lot of things bother her. She isn't comfortable with things she doesn't know or understand. She won't try to understand anything foreign to her way of life or thought. I don't even know what 'being Jewish' means." He answered.

"Look Noah, my people have been persecuted forever. If, no when, there is a war, we'll be blamed. I know it won't be easy for us," she said. She looked at him, studying him for a moment, then she smiled, "It's too nice a night to talk about such things. Let's go home."

She got up, still holding his hand, and then leaned over and kissed him on the cheek.

"Thanks," she said.

"For what?" he asked, flushed and confused.

"I don't know," she replied, "For just being here, for being you.

CHAPTER 5

Noah spent another fretful night with his dreams permeated by thoughts of Ann. It seemed to him that there were two sides to her; the young, pretty, exciting girl on the edge of womanhood, and the world-weary, fearful, old before her time, woman. It was this dichotomy that he found confusing, mixing with the emotional feelings surging within him. He had dated before, but nothing seriously. His only real experience had been with a girl from high school named Judy Sims, who had moved to town over the summer and entered school that fall. He thought he was in love. They had gone to the movies, the malt shop, and a few parties; she had even let him kiss her a few times, but nothing else. She had gone to the prom with one of the football players, breaking his heart. His friend David said she had just been using him to meet new people. After that, and through college, he stuck to his studies realizing he did not relate to the girls his own age that he found silly and self-absorbed. The few friends he had, with the exception of David, were always kidding him about "never getting to first base."

Ann had promised to help her aunt and could not see him this morning. Since he could not sleep, he decided to get dressed and go visit Sam. Sam lived in a small, neat, house at the edge of town near the base of the mountain. He was the only colored person in town and had lived there half his life. He was in his early forties and after lying about his age had served as a cook in the last war. When the conflict ended, he was mustered out and traveled around the country. He disliked larger cities or crowds of people so had eventually settled in the mountains, finding the environment he was seeking. He had found Fairview to be both friendly and warm to everyone. He liked it that people here accepted him as an equal and did not look down on him because of his skin color. He was grateful for that. Of all the places he had been, this was the only place where he felt truly at home.

Noah walked up the steps to the porch and noticed there was a pile of wood shavings under the old rocker where Sam, in between working odd jobs, would sit and whittle out the animal forms he sold to the tourists. Noah knocked on the door, causing Blu, Sam's hound dog, to begin barking.

"Shut up boy. Just a minute," Noah heard Sam say. He opened the door and when he saw Noah a huge grin stretched across his face. "Well if you ain't a sight for these ol' eyes. Come on in Mr. Noah," Sam said, reaching with his foot to push Blu away. "Get back Boy," he said. "Sit down, sit down." he said, pointing to one of the old upholstered chairs. "Good to see you. You're out awful early. Would you like something to eat?" Sam asked.

"No thanks, but I would take a cup of that coffee," Noah said, pointing to the pot on the stove.

Sam handed him a cup and Noah sat down on the old, well-worn chair. Blu limped over and curled up on a braided rug next to the stone fireplace. Noah studied Sam for a moment, noticing that he had not changed in the past year. He was still tall and his frame lean and muscular from working at various odd jobs. Streaks of gray were beginning to show on Sam's close-cropped hair. Sam held a special place in Noah's heart, perhaps because Sam always found time for him and treated him as an equal. Sam taught him so much about life and in so-doing, how to live as a man.

"What happened to Blu?" Noah asked.

"Not sure, but I think something got hold of him. He came limping in the other night with a gash on his leg. I think maybe it was a cat." Sam said.

"A cat?" Noah asked incredulously.

"A mountain lion," Sam said. "I heard one the other night. It's scary, sounds like a woman screaming. You need to be careful if you go up into the mountains."

"Yes sir, I will," Noah replied.

"You here for a few weeks?" Sam asked.

"Yeah," Noah replied. "We're all here; Michael, Mom, Dad and Thelma. They're all going back in a couple of weeks, but I'm staying for the whole summer."

"That's great. We'll be able to spend lots of time visiting. Who is Thelma?" Sam asked.

"She's Mom's housekeeper. Mom thought it would be easier on Granny if she came and helped," he said, "And on her," he thought. Another thought crossed his mind. "You'll have to meet her, she's really nice," Noah said.

"I'm sure she is," Sam replied. "Now tell me what you've been doing? How's your family?" Sam asked.

Noah assured him everyone was well and related the events of the previous year and then what had happened since he arrived.

Sam arched his eyebrow and he smiled as Noah began to tell him about Ann.

"Sure does sound like you've met a nice girl and one who might teach you a thing or two about fishing," Sam said with a laugh.

Noah got up and handed Sam the empty coffee cup. "I'd better be getting back," then added, "If it's okay, I'd like to bring Ann and Thelma over later to meet you."

"That would be real nice," Sam said. "I'd like to meet them too."

That afternoon after lunch, while everyone was resting, Noah took Thelma and Ann over to meet Sam. Sitting on the porch, they relished the afternoon breeze as Ann told them about Paris.

"I know a little about it," Sam interjected. "I spent some time there after the last war. Being colored never seemed to bother the French. I liked it very much. It's really old and pretty," he hesitated and then added, "and they sure have some beautiful women." Glancing at Thelma, he quickly injected, "but I still prefer American girls."

"It's really nice here," Thelma said, ignoring his comment.

"Not like home?" Sam asked.

"No, everything at home is flat land, mostly cotton. Believe me; I've picked many a bag. Picked it 'till my hands was bloody and my back felt permanently bent."

Sam studied her with a sorrowful eye. "Life ain't easy, Miss Thelma, but it's all we got. How about some lemonade?" Sam asked Thelma. "Why don't you help me?"

"Be glad to," Thelma said smiling, as she rose from her chair.

They went inside and Sam got out the pitcher and glasses, and began squeezing some lemons.

"They sure look nice together, Miss Thelma," Sam said thoughtfully as he peered out the window.

"Yes," Thelma answered. "She's really sweet. By the way, don't call me Miss. It's just Thelma."

"Yes Ma'am," he replied and then said, "I mean yes, Thelma."

"Sam, where's your sugar?" She asked.

He looked around, pointing at the cupboard. "It's in there. I keep forgetting where I put it, cause Doctor George says I'm not 'sposed to use it. My blood's too sweet."

Thelma opened the cupboard door and stared in amazement.

"Sam, what are you doing with all these cans of peaches?" She asked incredulously.

Sam looked at her sheepishly. "When I was young, my father was a sharecropper. We didn't have much. Once a week, on Saturday, I went with him to town to buy supplies. I would take the eggs in to sell and my father would give me a dime to buy a can of peaches. I would dream about those peaches all week and my mouth would start watering when I walked into that store. I'd open that can, reach in and fish them out one at a time, and then drink that sweet syrup, letting it run down my face. My father would laugh and make me go outside and wash up in the horse trough. I still remember those times with my father and the sweet taste of those peaches. I bought a bunch of them so I would never be out." He hesitated, then continued, "You know, Thelma, those peaches just don't taste as good as they did back then."

Thelma felt a catch in her throat, realizing for the first time that Sam was a special man. She hesitated before adding the sugar.

"Go ahead," Sam said, "I don't care what they say. All my life people been taken' away from me. The only thing I got left is the pleasure from the food I eats, and I'm sure not about to let them take that too."

They carried the lemonade back out on the porch. Thelma smiled as she noticed Ann and Noah holding hands.

That evening, Noah and Ann walked down to the lake and sat once again holding hands, taking in the beauty of their moon lit surroundings.

"Listen," Noah said.

"What?" Ann asked.

There was a soft splashing sound.

"That's a trout breaking the water, chasing bugs." Noah said.

He turned, looking into her eyes. "You know, Ann, I don't think there's any place on earth as peaceful as a mountain lake on a summer night." He said as he took in the beauty spread before them.

She studied him for a moment then said, "I really like you, Noah."

He noticed a tear on her cheek.

"Hey, don't cry. I like you too," he said.

"I'm...I'm crying because I'm happy," she said, smiling. Then, a serious look came over her face. "I don't want to lose this... you." She made an ark with her hand.

He touched her cheek and wiped the tear away.

"Don't be silly," he replied. "You won't lose me. I like you. I like you a lot."

She pointed at her chest then his. "Me too, you," she replied with a smile.

Noah could not help noticing the incredible depth her eyes possessed suddenly having the urge to kiss her, but in his hesitancy, he let the moment pass.

They sat quietly, watching the moonbeams dancing on the water, leaving strings of jewel-like patterns rippling across the lake. As it grew colder, Noah reached over and put his arm around Ann, pulling her to him.

"That feels good," she said.

"It feels right," Noah thought.

CHAPTER 6

He had to eat. It had been days and his strength was fading. He had been reduced to eating carrion, which he would never do if he were healthy. He went down to the stream to drink and to try to catch one of the water creatures that swam in the river. He was still thirsty and had been unsuccessful at catching a swimmer, although he had eaten a frog and a crayfish, neither of which he liked nor did little to stop his hunger.

Suddenly, he caught the scent of food mixed with the scent of a two-legged one. He cautiously worked his way upstream, staying in the brush by the water. It was still lighter than he preferred, but his stomach made him bold. He traveled about a quarter of a mile when he came to a clearing. There, he saw the two-legged bent over a rock, tearing into several swimmers.

He was delirious in his hunger. No matter what the consequences, he had to eat now. Slowly he worked his way closer, until he was only eight lengths away. He crouched, relaxed, with his tail slowly waving. He sniffed the air and rotated his ears. His senses detected nothing except the two-leg, the swimmers and the smell from the fire near the lair of the two-leg.

He knew he had to act fast, or he might not have the strength. He coiled into a crouch and summoned up what was left of the energy stored in his spine. Suddenly, he released that power and sprang forward, propelled by the powerful muscles of his hindquarters, his thick tail acting as a counterbalance.

When he was on his prey, he extended his claws and reached out with both massive forepaws, getting a solid grip on the two-legs' neck and shoulder.

Usually the impact was enough to break his prey's neck, but to make sure, he bit hard into the back of the neck forcing his long, slender, canines between the vertebrae, severing the spinal cord.

The attack weakened him and he stopped to rest for a moment. To gain strength, he ate the several small swimmers next to the two-leg. He then turned to eating the two-leg, plucking at the strange skin and hair of its body. Even though tough and matted, he succeeded in making an opening. He ripped into the body cavity and began eating the highly nutritious heart, liver and lungs. He could feel his strength returning. He moved on to the meaty hindquarters. He ate about twenty pounds before his hunger was temporarily satiated.

Dragging the carcass into the bushes, he used his front paws to rake dirt, grass and leaves over the remains to hide it from scavengers. He moved back into the brush finding a concealed location to rest and groom himself. The warm weather would spoil the meat soon, so he would not wait too long before feeding again. For the first time since that night with the thunder stick, he felt good. He could feel his strength returning and instinctively realized he would again attack this new, easy source of prey.

The next afternoon Noah and Ann decided to go to her uncle's drugstore for sodas. Ira Zimmerman was behind the counter in back, filling prescriptions. Ann waved to her uncle and then led Noah over to the soda fountain.

"Hi Ted," Ann said to the young soda jerk.

"Hi Ann," he said.

"Ted, this is Noah Johnson. He's staying with Doctor Johnson," she said.

"Hi," he answered, holding out his hand. "Ted Martin. Glad to meet you."

Noah nodded and replied with his own, "Hello," and shook Teds hand.

"Come meet my uncle," Ann said. "Ted, bring us two chocolate sodas, please."

She led Noah to the back where Mr. Zimmerman was behind the prescription counter surrounded by shelves filled with boxes and bottles of various ointments, pills and elixirs. Mr. Zimmerman was short and thin and he wore a starched white shirt and bow tie. Noah noticed he had eyes like Ann's, even though they were covered by wire-framed glasses. "Uncle, this is Noah Johnson." Ann said.

"Yes, I know. You're the young man who's staying at Doctor Johnson's. I'm glad to meet you. My niece has said nice things about you." He said, extending his hand to Noah.

Noah noticed the reddening on Ann's face.

"I understand you visit them each summer?" Mr. Zimmerman asked.

"Yes sir." Noah answered.

"I certainly like your Grandfather. We are really lucky to have him here." Mr. Zimmerman said.

"Thank you," Noah responded.

"Uncle, we're going to have a soda," Ann said.

"Nice to meet you Mr. Zimmerman," Noah said, feeling more at ease by her uncle's demeanor. He led Ann back to the front where they sat down at a table.

"Your uncle seems nice enough." Noah said.

"He's a little old-fashioned and set in his ways, but really caring. My aunt says that I have him wrapped around my finger," she said with a laugh.

Noah certainly understood how that could happen.

Ted brought their sodas over to them. "Enjoy," Ted said.

"Thanks," Noah answered.

The bell at the store's front door tinkled, as someone entered.

"Whoa." Ted said suddenly.

"What?" Noah asked.

"Eugene 'Bogey' Harris," Ted said, motioning with his eyes toward the front of the store.

"Who's Bogey Harris?" Noah asked.

"Trouble," Ted said. "He's a local bully, thinks he's real cool, like Humphrey Bogart. He lives outside of town with his drunk of a father. His mother left long ago, supposedly with a fisherman from upstate. Bogey dropped out of school several years ago and spends his time making life miserable for everyone he comes in contact with around here."

Noah studied Bogey as he approached the soda fountain. He was of average height with short powerful arms and close-set eyes on a round face that gave him almost a pig-like appearance. His smirk mirrored the hatred and pain within him

"Give me a Coke," he ordered, as Ted walked back around the counter.

He sat at the counter, watching Noah and Ann. Ann got up to go to the bathroom and Bogey walked over to Noah.

"Hey, you messing around with that Jew?" he asked. Noah was momentarily taken by surprise and then chose not to answer. "I'm talking to you, boy. You don't want to be messin' with a Jew now do you?" Noah tried to ignore him. Bogey pounded his fist on the table. "Answer me."

"Yeah, I do," Noah said.

"Boy, you don't want to do that. I seen you with that nigger, too," Bogey said.

"Looks like you're drinking a Jew's coke," Noah said pointing to Bogey's glass.

"Smartass. Don't fuck with me." He took the drink and poured it on the table, turning to leave, holding up his middle finger. "I'll be seeing you," he said.

Noah sat in shocked silence watching Bogey leave. He had a momentary vision of his mother washing his mouth out with soap.

"What was that about?" Ann asked as she returned.

"Nothing, he just spilled his drink." Noah said as he took a handful of napkins and wiped up the mess. They finished their sodas and got up to leave. "Nice to meet you, Ted," Noah said on their way out.

"Yeah," Ted said, and then motioned Noah over speaking quietly, "Watch him. You don't want to piss him off."

"Thanks. I'll be careful," Noah whispered, then turned towards the back of the store and waved. "Goodbye, Mr. Zimmerman."

"Goodbye, son," he said, as they went out the door.

It began to rain as they left the drug store, one of those late afternoon showers that happen often in the mountains during summer. Not wanting to go back into the store, they sat down on a bench under the awning, watching the rain.

"You know when I was a kid, I would sit on my porch when it rained and pretend I was the captain of a ship, fighting the storm, trying to save the vessel and all aboard," Noah said.

"You pretended a lot. You must have been lonely," Ann said.

"Yeah, I guess I was. I never played sports. Just read a lot and made make believe. Later, a boy my age moved next door. His name was David. We were nothing alike. He was athletic and very social and yet we became friends. We went through school together and then I went on to college and he went to work at home. He's still my only real friend."

"I'm your friend." She exclaimed.

"I know," he said, turning to look at her, "Thanks." He couldn't help thinking she was becoming much more than, 'a friend'

"What about girlfriends?" Ann asked.

"I never was good with girls. I just couldn't relax and carry on a conversation." He said.

"You're good around me," she said.

"I know, but you're different." He said.

"How? I'm a girl." She said indignantly.

Noah laughed then answered hesitantly, "I think it's because I feel comfortable with you. I'm relaxed around you; I can be myself and not try to be something I'm not."

"Thanks a lot," she said with an air of anger. "You make me sound like an old shoe."

Noah was taken aback. "I'm sorry, I didn't mean it. I…"

This time she laughed, "I'm just teasing. I know what you mean. It's the same with me. My parents would only allow me to date Jewish boys, and they had to be from the right families. I was miserable. Nothing would ever come of it because I resented them, even if it wasn't their fault."

"Tell me about your family," Noah said. "You know a lot about mine but I know almost nothing about yours. For instance, you said your father was in banking?"

"Yes, he is a partner in a bank in Paris." Ann said. "He has worked there since college." She hesitated then added, "I wish he didn't work so hard. He is gone so often that I don't get to see him much."

"I'm sorry. What about your mother?" Noah asked.

"They got married right out of school and she has been a homemaker ever since. She was interested in fashion and might have worked in that area but my father wanted her to stay home and start a family. She didn't argue and any opportunity passed when she became pregnant with me and later my sister. She occasionally does some social activities like taking care of the infirmed and working with women's groups."

"What is your sister like?" Noah asked.

"We are alike in a lot of ways, but she is really pretty and smart. She is interested in fashion like my mother while I'm more into art and music. In any case we are lucky to be living in Paris where the opportunities in fashion, music and art are plentiful." She hesitated, then she added, with a feeling of sadness, "That is, if we don't get into a war."

She paused for a moment then said, "Just a minute, I want to show you something," she then got up and went into the drug store. She returned carrying a photograph.

"This is my family." She said handing him the picture.

He looked at it carefully studying the faces in the photo. There was a well-dressed, older, rather portly man sporting a beard. A woman, who looked like an aged, somewhat shorter, and heavier version of Ann, and a young girl, who he realized must be her younger sister, Rachel. She was shorter than Ann, and still possessed a girlish quality. Noah could see she was on the verge of blossoming into a beautiful young woman. He was mesmerized by Ann; she looked as pretty as she did now.

"That was taken last year. I miss them so. I wish they were here with me, with us, safe in these mountains." She said solemnly.

As Noah studied her, he suddenly realized how much more she was beginning to mean to him. "I do too," he said, putting his arm around her. The rain stopped and Noah walked Ann home. He reached down and took her hand in his remarking to himself how natural it felt.

CHAPTER 7

It was the Fourth of July and Fairview was celebrating with a grand picnic and day in the park. The Depression had hit hard here, just as it had the rest of the country, but the New Deal was beginning to work and there was a spirit of optimism; a sense that good times were ahead. George explained to Noah and Ann that there would be a covered dish lunch followed by games like sack races and tug-of-war, then, later that night a dance, ending in fireworks.

Noah was excited about the day's activities. He and Ann had been almost inseparable the last ten days, spending all their spare time together, enjoying each other's company and the beauty of the world that surrounded them. Noah, with his grandparents' permission, invited the Zimmerman's to join their group. Thelma and Sam were also invited. Louise had protested inviting the Zimmerman's, but gave up after Thelma and Sam were included.

Mary and Thelma got up early to fry chicken and make potato salad to go with the loaf of homemade bread and a cherry pie they had baked. Sam sniffed the wonderful aroma as he walked into the kitchen.

"Boy it sure smells good in here." Sam said.

"Yeah, and stay away, 'cause smelling it is all you're going to get to do till we all sit down to enjoy it," Thelma said, trying hard not to show how glad she was to see him. They had been spending time together when they could, and she was growing very fond of this man.

He smiled at Thelma. "Doctor George said since he had to tend to some patients, for me to come over and see if there was something I could help with," he said to Mary.

"You can get that big pot over there and fill it with water so we can boil the potatoes," Mary instructed.

"Yes, ma'am," Sam said. As he walked passed Thelma, he gave her a pat on the rear; she turned and hit him with a wooden spoon she was holding.

"You two love birds cut it out or we'll never get this food ready," Mary said.

Thelma made a shooing motion at Sam, turning away so he would not notice the darkening color of her face. They had been seeing each other, but had tried to keep it a secret.

Arthur walked in. "Good morning," he said.

"Where's Louise?" Mary asked.

"She's still asleep. Shall I wake her?" Arthur asked.

"No no, don't do that. We've got everything under control." Mary said.

"Where're the boys?" Arthur asked.

"Noah went to help Ann over at the Zimmerman's. George and Michael went down to Mr. Hartley's store to buy fireworks," Mary said.

Just then the door burst open and Michael bounded in holding up his booty.

"Hey everybody!" he said excitedly.

"What you got there?" Sam said, pointing to the sack.

"I got sparklers, firecrackers, and roman candles. Boy is it going to be fun!" Michael said, grinning from ear to ear.

Everyone in Fairview gathered at the lake. Four long picnic tables were put end to end with all the food placed on them. Joseph Hartley filled five number three washtubs with watermelons and ice. A group of men had gathered around six ice cream freezers and were taking turns cranking the handles. A group of young children took turns sitting on top, enjoying the cold, and keeping the dasher from floating up.

Noah and Ann competed in the sack race. They each put one leg in a burlap feed bag and then put their arms around each other, which Noah found very pleasurable. Half-way through the race they fell, and Noah landed on top of Ann. For a moment they both laughed, but then became silent as they stared into each other's eyes. Reluctantly, Noah got up and gave Ann a hand up. Next, they tried the egg toss but did not last long. On their third try the egg broke. Later they had a good laugh when they heard the winner had been disqualified for using a hardboiled egg. Sam tried his hand at the anvil throw, which he won, and then the tug-of-war while Michael was having a great time throwing firecrackers at the feet of several girls.

"If I can have your attention," Joseph Hartley said. "Thank you. Gather' round, please. As Mayor of Fairview, I want to welcome each of you. It seems that for the first time in several years, we have something to celebrate. There is turmoil in other parts of the world, but here in America it seems our future is looking brighter. That fair in Chicago is touting the World of Tomorrow and it sure looks good for us, so everyone enjoy themselves. I'm going to ask Preacher Harris to give our blessing so we can eat."

After the Methodist minister, John Harris, gave the blessing, everyone migrated to the tables to fill their plates with the food they each had contributed.

"I bet I'll see a lot of these kids in the office tomorrow with stomach aches," George said.

"Boy, there sure is a lot of food," said Michael, gazing over the tables.

"Yes, there is, but that doesn't mean you have to eat all of it," Louise said.
"Did you wash your hands?" she asked.

"Yes ma'am," Michael answered, even though he had not.

"Where is Noah?" she asked.

"He's over there with Ann and the Zimmerman's," Michael said, pointing.

"Tell him, them, to join us over by that tree," she said, showing him where. "Arthur, come on, let's eat."

The Zimmerman's joined them under the tree, where several blankets were spread out. Thelma and Sam had gone a little way off to be by themselves, knowing that their presence would make Louise uncomfortable. Louise and Mary spread out the cloth, and set out the dishes and food. Michael reached for a piece of chicken.

"Hold on, we haven't said the blessing," Louise said. Then she paused and looked at the Zimmerman's.

"It's ok, we believe in God, too," Ira said. George gave the blessing, being careful not to mention Jesus. Noah refused the chicken as he always did, ever since the time his pet rooster Blackie had disappeared, only to show up on the dinner table as the main course.

They ate as if they would not be given another chance, then lay back on the blankets and let the warmth of the sun and the gentle mountain breeze do its work. Louise began talking about movies she wanted to see. She talked about Gone with the Wind and a new movie coming out starring Judy Garland from the book The Wonderful Wizard of Oz. George started telling about a book he was reading, How Green Was My Valley. As he began a synopsis of it, Louise made a face.

"Oh, that sounds so boring and depressing," she said. George just shook his head and reached for his pipe.

Noah got up, reached out and took Ann's hand, helping her to stand. They walked towards the lake, searching for a secluded spot away from the crowds, and sat down. Noah once again took Ann's hand.

"I think I know what I want to do with my life," he said.

"What," she asked.

"I want to become a doctor and come back here to practice." He turned and took Ann in his arms. "I love it here. I really don't want to live anyplace else. Grandfather's getting old. I could come back here and eventually take over his practice. Besides, I've never been up here in the winter. It would certainly be different. What do you think"? He asked.

"I think, no, I know I love you and I think it's a great plan." She said.

"What did you say?" He asked.

"I said I think it would be a good thing." She replied.

"No, the other." He asked.

Ann turned to him, "I said I love you."

"Oh Ann, I love you too. My life would be complete if you were here with me," he said. He leaned over and began to kiss her; all his fears and apprehensions gone.

Soon they were touching and kissing, oblivious to their surroundings. Suddenly, there was a rustling sound behind them. They turned quickly; Noah thought it might be an animal.

"Well, what do we have here?" asked Bogey Harris, as he stepped from behind a bush.

"Bogey, what are you doing?" Noah asked obviously relieved and irritated at the same time.

"I might ask you the same thing." Bogey replied with a sneer.

"Why don't you leave us alone?" Ann said angrily.

"Oh, listen to the Jew bitch," Bogey said taunting Noah.

"What do you want?" Noah asked, exasperated.

"Might want some of that," Bogey said, pointing to Ann.

"Aren't you afraid you might catch some Jewish disease?" Ann asked, sarcastically.

"Cute," Bogey said.

"Look Bogey, you've had your fun. Why don't you just get out of here and leave us alone?" Noah said.

"Oh, like you're going to make me," Bogey said, hands on his hips.

"No, he won't. But I will." Came a familiar voice.

They all turned to see Sam and Thelma standing at the edge of the clearing. Bogey stared at Sam and then looked back at Noah.

"I'll see you and your Jewish bitch later," he said. He turned, holding up his middle finger as he walked away. "Fuck all of you." Bogey spat.

"Thanks, Sam," Noah said, relieved.

"No problem. I saw him headed your way so I thought I'd better check. That boy sure is full of anger, he's like a snake all coiled up ready to strike, ain't nothing good gonna' come from him. You need to be careful."

"Yeah, you're right." Noah nodded, and couldn't help thinking this was the second time he had been warned.

That evening everyone gathered by the gazebo to watch the fireworks and listen to the band play. Michael was running around lighting sparklers and shooting Roman Candles.

"Be careful," Louise admonished, with a note of worry. "Arthur, make him come back here," she said.

"Leave him alone, he's okay. Let him have fun," Noah said. He looked at his father, wishing he would stand up to her just once. Suddenly the sky was lit by a riot of color and sound. Everyone was oohing and ahhing, except Ann. Noah noticed she was crying.

"What's the matter?" He asked, putting his arm around her. "I don't know." she pointed at the sky, "I think it's because those remind me of cannon fire."

"Darling, please don't. There are still things that are beautiful and have nothing to do with war," Noah said.

"I know," she said, hugging him. "I'll try. Maybe you can be my eyes, and I can see the world like you do, from the safety of your arms.

CHAPTER 8

The two weeks passed quickly and it was time for Noah's family to leave. They were leaving the next morning and would return at the end of summer. Arthur had to get back to the store and Louise was going, as she put it, "stir crazy". Michael wanted to see his friends. Thelma was the only one who wanted to stay, largely because of her newfound friendship with Sam. She talked to Mary and was able to enlist her help in convincing Louise that she was needed to keep an eye on Noah and to help Mary around the house. To the amazement of both of them, Louise said that she thought it was a good idea.

Mary decided that they would have a going away party that evening. Noah suggested to his mother that he and George go fishing in order to have some fresh fish to eat. Secretly he just wanted to get away and spend some time with Ann and his Grandfather. She acquiesced and Noah wasted no time in rounding up George and then stopping at Ann's, where he talked Mrs. Zimmerman into letting Ann and Beau go along.

It was a perfect mountain day - blue skies, wispy soft white clouds, and a gentle breeze ruffling the myriad flowers in the meadow.

"Man, those fish are really going to be biting," Noah said.

George just said, "Yep."

They arrived at the spot where they had so much luck before. Noah did not waste any time starting to fish. Ann sat down on a rock and petted Beau saying she was just going to watch them, since she didn't want to show up Noah.

They had been fishing for over an hour with no success when suddenly Beau started to become agitated. He began to bark, then whine and fidget. Ann kept trying to calm him. "Something's bothering Beau," she said.

"Probably just a rabbit or squirrel," George said, raising his head.

He had heard the two legs and began to work his way towards them. Crouching in the brush and trees, he slowly edged his way closer so he could see them. He had finished off what was left of the two-leg from several days ago and was ready to eat again. He studied them from his concealment; there were many of them and a barker. He was not hungry enough yet to take them all on.

"Hush, Beau," Ann said.

"I think we might as well call it a day," George said.

"Let me try a few more casts," Noah said. He had caught one fish which was so small he released it.

George let him cast a few more times to no avail and then said, "Let's go Noah."

Noah looked sullen and George could tell he wasn't happy.

"Hey Noah, don't be so glum. Sometimes things don't work out like we planned. I know you wanted to catch a lot of fish, but you know the day isn't wasted." He looked around, motioning with his hands. "Just look at all this beauty around us. Listen to the music of the water and the wind." He bent down and picked up a handful of soil and held it to his nose. "Smell the fragrance of the earth and flowers, and just enjoy being alive here in the company of each other. You know, Noah, all in all, I'd say our creel is pretty full." George reached down and patted Beau's head, helped Ann up and putting his arm around.

Noah said "Let's go home."

He watched them leave, and somewhere in his feline brain the thought came to him that they would be back. All he had to do was watch and wait.

"Noah, come here a minute, please," George asked.

Noah came into the study where his grandfather was busy tying flies. He held one up for Noah to look at. "What do you think?" He asked.

"Boy, they sure look natural. I almost expect them to fly away," Noah said in amazement.

"You know, I think tying these flies has strengthened my belief that there is a God." George said. "Try as I might, whatever I create is but a poor imitation of the wonder that is the real thing." He said in adoration.

George asked Noah if he would mind taking some of the flies he had tied over to Mr. Hartley's store. Noah agreed, and left for the general store.

When he walked in, Mr. Hartley was talking on the phone. "Yes sir. I'll keep an eye out in case he comes in here Sheriff. Probably lost track of time. It happens if the fishing is really good. I'll ask around…see if anyone else may have seen him. Might have left and just didn't bother to check in. Sure, I'll be happy to put up a notice. Okay, Sheriff, you too. Goodbye."

"Hi, Noah," Mr. Hartley said after hanging up the phone.

"Hello, Mr. Hartley." Noah answered.

"What can I do for you?" Mr. Hartley asked

"Granddad asked me to bring you these flies he's been tying," Noah said, holding out a box full of colorful imitations of the insects and aquatic life that George had fashioned from feathers, cloth, and string.

"Won't have a problem selling these. Doc sure does make some beautiful patterns," Mr. Hartley said, admiring George's creations.

Noah nodded in agreement and then began to look around the store. In one of the display cases something caught his eye and he walked over to look at it.

"Can I show you something, Noah?"

"May I see that medallion?" Noah asked, pointing to the case.

"That's a nice one, sterling silver, with a sterling chain. The two hearts can each be engraved with a name and there's room on the back for anything else," Mr. Hartley replied as he handed it to him. "You thinkin' about giving it to anyone special? Wouldn't be that Ann Meyer I've seen you with, would it?" he asked with a grin.

Noah didn't answer. He just looked at the medallion then handed it back and thanked Mr. Hartley.

"She's really nice and a very pretty girl," Mr. Hartley said reassuringly. Noah nodded again and then turned to leave, lost in thought.

"Noah, tell you what, I'll keep this for you for a few days, just in case you decide you want to give it to someone," Mr. Hartley said, placing the medallion in a drawer under the counter.

Noah left Mr. Hartley's and headed to Ira Zimmerman's Drug store, hoping to see Ann. He walked in and looked around.

"She's not here. She's helping Ruth … err Mrs. Zimmerman," Mr. Zimmerman said.

"Thanks," Noah said, and left the store.

He thought he might go visit Sam and started that way. He had only gone a little way when he saw 'Bogey' Harris and two of his friends.

"Well if it ain't my friend, Noah Johnson," Bogey said, with a sneer.

"Hi Bogey," Noah replied, knowing better than to call him Eugene.

"What've you been doing?" Bogey asked, with a sneer as he turned to his companions. He mockingly asked, "What do you boys think he's been doing, or maybe it's who he's been doing." Bogey turned to Noah again and stared menacingly at Noah. Noah tensed, as Bogey slowly walked toward him. "I bet I know. He's been hanging out with that nigger friend of his and screwing around with that little Jew bitch. Hitler's right, we need to get rid of all that scum," Bogeys voice increased in intensity until he was yelling and then he spit, as he continued toward Noah.

Noah could not control the anger that welled up in him. He turned and punched Bogey in the face. Bogey, stunned for a moment, began to hit back. Bogey's friends grabbed Noah and held him while Bogey flailed away.

"What are you going to do now, nigger lover, Jew lover?" Bogey and his friends hollered over and over. Noah finally fell to the ground, as they kicked him, spat on him and kicked dirt on him. Finally, their fury vented, they walked away.

Noah lay there in the dirt for a while and then stumbled to his feet. He did not want to go home looking like he did, so he headed over to Sam's.

Sam opened the door took one look at Noah and gasped, "What happened? You okay?" Sam asked with great concern.

"Yeah," Noah replied through puffy lips, not wanting to reveal how he really felt.

Sam helped him in and began tending to his injuries. Noah's clothes were torn and dirty. He had blood on his nose and lips, as well as scrapes, cuts, and bruises on his face and limbs.

"What happened?" Sam asked again.

Noah shook his head, indicating he would not say.

"Lord, Noah," Sam said, "If you're not a sorry sight. It would be easier for your Mother to have another kid than to try and clean you up." Sam exclaimed.

Noah, with Sam's help, managed to clean up his cuts and scrapes. Sam wrapped some ice in a towel and had Noah hold it on his face. They found a shirt to replace the torn one Noah wore. Finally, Noah thanked Sam and started out the door for home.

"I'll walk with you," Sam said.

"No, I'll be all right," Noah said.

"I'd really like to. To tell you the truth, I need an excuse to see Miss Thelma again. I sure like her." Sam said with a sheepish grin.

"Yeah, she likes you too," Noah added.

When they made it back to the house, Sam went to the back door and whispered to Thelma through the screen and told her what had happened. Noah wanted to avoid his parents and asked Thelma to fetch his grandfather without alerting the rest of the family. George was shocked to see Noah looking like he did.

"What happened?" George asked in astonishment and concern.

Noah asked his Grandfather if he could talk to him in private. "I don't want anyone else to know," Noah said.

"Come in here," George said, taking Noah into the study, "It's okay now. This'll be our secret," George replied.

They sat down and Noah told his grandfather everything that happened. When he finished, he said in a hushed tone, "I'm going to get even with him." Noah said, with resolve.

George walked to the window, looking out at the landscape for a moment. Turning back facing Noah, he said, "Noah, the world's always going to have a few frightened people that are so full of despair, loneliness, and helplessness that all they can do is take it out on others. We can't let them pull us down to their level. Come here," he said, walking over to where Mary was working on a quilt that was stretched on a frame.

Pointing at it, he said, "See that?"

"Uh, yeah," replied Noah, questioning.

"Look closely, what do you see?" George asked.

Noah hesitated, thinking about his response. "I see a quilt with a lot of different pieces and colors."

"You're right, but there's more to it," George said. "It's made up of a lot of different fabric, each one a different pattern, color, and shape, but there's one thing that holds them together. Do you know what that is?" George asked.

Noah shook his head no. "It's the thread. The same thing is true of us, Noah. We're all different colors, patterns, and shapes. Our beliefs and backgrounds are different, but we're all held together by the common thread of our humanity, our belief in a higher power and in the innate goodness of our fellow man. Do you understand what I'm saying?" George asked.

"Yes sir, I think so," Noah said.

George reached over and tousled Noah's hair. He looked at Noah for a moment then said, "I love you, Noah."

"I love you too, Grandpa," Noah replied, smiling.

His grandfather winked at him and said in a voice loud enough for everyone to hear. "By the way, Noah, you are going to have to be a lot more careful where you step when you go hiking. Can't have you keep continuing to fall down. Next time you might really hurt yourself." Said George.

The next morning Noah got up in time to see his parents and Michael off. His father wanted to get an early start to avoid the afternoon heat. Noah, still sore and cut up, stuck to his story that he had been hiking and did not pay attention to where he was walking. He explained that he had tripped over a root and fallen down an embankment. George assured Noah's parents that there was no reason for them to delay their departure. Noah, he told them, would be okay, and having learned a valuable lesson, would be more mindful in the future.

His mother pretended to worry about him, warning him to be careful, but he knew it was mostly for show. It was what mothers were supposed to do. She acted as though she was going to miss Thelma very much, but again Noah felt that his mother had a newfound sense of freedom and was glad Thelma was staying behind. She would still hire a part time housekeeper. Michael was going to work with his Dad at the grocery store after school and when he wasn't involved in football. Louise would be able to do all the volunteer and social work, not to mention shopping, she wanted. It seemed to Noah that she was positively glowing.

The party the night before had been a letdown. Noah was not allowed to invite Ann, since his mother said she wanted just family. Thelma would have liked to invite Sam but knew that Louise would stick to her decision and opted not to bring it up. They had no fish, so Thelma and Mary served a ham that one of George's patients had cured. Noah ate a little of it, but thought it was too salty. Thelma baked biscuits and Mary opened a jar of her home canned apple butter. They had fresh green beans and a blackberry cobbler from berries Mrs. Zimmerman had sent over by Ann. Louise had examined them after Ann left. Arthur watched her for a minute, and then told her not to worry; cooking would kill anything Jewish on them. He noticed she actually seemed relieved.

They had eaten in relative silence. Much to the chagrin of Louise, Mary invited Thelma to sit with them. It seemed to Noah that his mother was uneasy through the whole meal. Later Noah overheard his parents talking.

"I can't believe she invited Thelma to sit with us," Louise said with an air of disgust.

"Why not, she practically raised the boys. She's probably been with them more than you," Arthur replied, trying not to show his disgust at his wife's bigotry.

"Oh Arthur, you know that's simply not true."

"Louise, I love you, but sometimes I feel you don't have a clue as to what life is really about." Arthur said wearily.

"What do you mean?" Louise asked with a puzzled expression.

He studied her for a moment then shook his head "Never mind. Let's just forget it. We need to finish packing. I want to get an early start tomorrow."

Noah was secretly glad to see them go, even though he loved them. Their departure seemed to raise a weight from him. He had a new felt sense of freedom. With Michael gone he also had his own room. Thelma was moved into his parents' room, something she was glad to do. Her back was hurting from sleeping on the cot, even though she never complained.

The next morning, as soon as Noah's parents left, Thelma went to see Sam. As she approached she could hear a woman singing in a throaty voice. Walking up on the porch, Sam met her at the door. "Come on in Thelma," Sam said.

"I heard the music," Thelma said, motioning to the record player. Sam walked over and cranked it some more. "That's Billie Holliday. Listen to that woman. She's been hurt so much by life you can feel the pain in her voice." He said.

Thelma looked at Sam, and at that moment realized the true depth of her feelings for him.

CHAPTER 9

Noah was almost giddy with his new-found freedom and knew exactly what he wanted to do. "Let's go on a picnic," he said to Ann, as he stood before her grinning from ear to ear.

"Are you sure you're, all right?" Ann asked, quizzically.

"Yeah, I'm fine," he said. He had told her the same story he told his parents. In Ann's case, it was to keep her from worrying. With their plans made, Ann, Thelma and Mary prepared the food and packed the basket.

They walked hand in hand through the meadow, which was filled with sunflowers, paintbrush, columbine, larkspur, lilies and many other flowers that formed a fragrant carpet in a riot of colors rippling in the wind, all framed by the snowcapped mountains and azure blue sky.

They took to the familiar trail, following the stream that flowed down the mountain and near the rock that was their special place. In the past, he had always hurried up the trail, wanting to reach the rock as soon as possible. Now he found himself lingering along the way, wanting to absorb all of the beauty around them. It was as if he was seeing it for the first time, and he was enthralled by the lyrical sound the stream made as it spilled and gurgled on its way to the lake. He looked back down the valley, and seeing a rainbow arching over it, pointed it out to Ann. "Look at that rainbow. When I was a kid I always wanted to find the pot of gold at its end." He exclaimed.

"I think you've found it," Ann said wistfully.

"What do you mean?" Noah asked quizzically.

"All this," she said with a sweep of her hand. "Oh Noah, it's so beautiful."

"It is beautiful," he said, looking at her. "And so are you." He said, unable to mask his love for her.

She squeezed his hand, smiled, then leaned over and kissed him.

When they reached the rock, they selected a copse of trees, spread their throw on the ground and sat down. They had left Beau at home, using the excuse of not wanting to have to watch him around the food.

"Let's eat," she said. They spread the food out on the cloth.

"I saw some wild strawberries over there," he said, standing up and pointing downstream.

"Are they good to eat?" She asked.

"You bet, the bears love them," he cupped his hands over his mouth and made a growling sound. Ann laughed and Noah reached down to help her up.

They walked over to the bushes and quickly gathered a cupful.

"These are the best strawberries I've ever eaten!" Ann exclaimed.

"It's this," Noah waved his arms at their surroundings, "that makes them taste so good."

After they finished eating, they lay down, side by side on the throw. Noah reached into the basket, pulled out a copy of The Prophet by Kahlil Gibran, and began to read.

> Love has no other desire but to fulfill itself.
> But if you love and must needs have desires,
> let these be your desires:
> to melt and be like a running brook that sings
> its melody to the night.
> To know the pain of too much tenderness.
> To be wounded by your own understanding
> of love: and to bleed willingly and joyfully.
> To wake at dawn with a winged heart and
> give thanks for another day of loving:
> to rest at the noon hour and meditate love's
> ecstasy.
> To return home at eventide with
> gratitude; and then to sleep with a prayer for
> the beloved in your heart and a song of praise upon your lips.

He finished, set the book back into the basket and turned on his side facing Ann. An incredible sense of awe came over him as he sensed the growing depth of his love.

"Oh Noah, that was wonderful. I go to sleep every night with a prayer on my lips for you, for us." She rolled on her side and putting her arms around him, gave him a long, lingering kiss. "I love you so." As they lay on the blanket, the heat of the day began to work its potion upon them and soon they drifted off into sleep.

Noah," Ann said softly, then realized she had awakened him. "I'm sorry; I didn't mean to wake you. I was just thinking out loud. Look at those clouds," she pointed at the sky. "Have you ever wondered if those same clouds are seen all over the world? I mean, here we are in this beautiful, peaceful place with those clouds above us just lazily traveling along without a care while on the other side of the world there is a war about to begin. Oh, Noah," she sobbed, "if only those same clouds could bring the beauty, peace, and love to my world that I know here in yours."

Noah hesitated before answering, "It's now your world here, too, Ann."

"If only it were," she replied. She turned on her side and looked at him. "Hold me Noah." She moved closer anticipating the warmth of his embrace.

He rolled closer and put his arms around her, pulling her close, kissing her.

"It's all right Ann," he said between kisses, "you're safe here with me."

"I can't hide and neither can you," she said. "If war breaks out, we'll all be affected, even you, even this country, this place. Noah I'm so afraid." She paused then said, "Tell me you love me."

"I love you," he said and then added, "I'll love you forever, and a day."

"Love me, Noah." Ann said with absolute resolve.

He was puzzled for a moment by her repetition and then it dawned on him what she was asking. "Ann....are you sure?"

"Oh, Noah, yes, yes I'm sure. I have to have something to hold on to, to hope about."

He began to kiss her lips, her cheeks, her eyes, her throat, her breasts, and it seemed as if the world, with all its cares and hurting stood still for that moment in time. He wasn't sure what he was supposed to do, and soon realized she wasn't, either, but in this Eden like setting, just like that first couple so long ago, they found their way together.

They lay, holding each other, looking up at the clouds. Noah turned his head toward her. "Are you, all right?" he asked. She squeezed him, nodding her head.

"What if you become pregnant?" Noah asked anxiously.

"Then it's God's will." She said.

"Ann?" He asked.

"Yes?" She said.

"Marry me!" He exclaimed, looking longingly at her.

"Yes, yes Noah, I will marry you when everything is back to normal." Ann said, turning to look at him.

"But there's no reason to wait. I can work for my father. We can live at home or we can stay here and I'll get a job." Noah said.

She kissed him again, "Noah, listen. The world's in a big mess. I don't know what will happen, but I know that it's going to get worse before it gets better. Let's enjoy this time together and then go from there. Noah?"

"Yes." He said.

"I'll love you forever," she smiled, and kissed him.

"And a day?" He asked, smiling in return

"And a day," she said, and kissed him once more.

He watched from the edge of the meadow, hidden in the shadows. His hunger was strong and he knew he had to eat soon. There were two of them and he watched as they sat by the stream under the trees. At first he thought they were fighting, but then his senses told him that they were mating. He waited, his ears moving in all directions listening for any unusual sounds. Just as he began to tense for his charge, he heard a noise. It was a barker. He relaxed, pressing back down to the ground. The barker was followed by a two leg, both of whom were heading towards the two under the trees. He would have to forget about them and search elsewhere.

They had dressed and were gathering up their picnic items when suddenly Beau came running up to them.

"Hey, where'd you come from?" Noah asked. He rubbed Beau's head vigorously. "Couldn't stand it, eh? Just had to join us." Ann laughed as Beau did a dance around them.

"Hey kids." They looked up, to see George. "Beau got out, so I thought I'd go look for him." He held up his fly rod. "Figured while I was out I'd try my luck." George could sense something was wrong. He studied Noah and Ann for a few moments. "Okay, what's the matter? He asked.

Noah glanced quickly at Ann, then back to George.

"Granddad, I asked Ann to marry me…but she refused, at least for now." Noah said.

George said nothing, but Noah thought he could detect a slight expression of disappointment on his face.

George set down his fly rod and turned to Ann.

"Why did you turn down the proposal?" He asked. After she told him her thoughts and relayed her fears, he thoughtfully said, "That's very sensible, but you know sometimes it's not the sensible, safe choices that make the difference. Life is not always sensible. Sometimes we have to swim against the current." He looked around and pointed up at the mountainside. "See the little trees growing up there in those cracks in the rocks?" They both looked to where he was pointing and nodded yes.

"There's something about those trees growing in that hostile environment that gives me hope. You see those little trees are stunted because of the harsh conditions in which they live. But they live and they are as green as any tree in the deepest, richest soil. They're doing what they are supposed to do, not complaining about their harsh environment, but doing everything in their power to live and grow and make that spot a little better place for other trees and plants in the years to come. By all rights, they should simply give up and recognize that theirs is no world where a tree can grow. But they don't. They go right on doing what trees do. They keep cracking rock and adding organic matter to make a little topsoil, they purify the air around them and each fall they add the beauty of their colors to the world. You see no matter what happens to the rest of the world, the air around those little trees will be cleaner and better, the soil will be richer, and the space around them will be prettier, simply because those trees won't give up. They make their contribution on the side of life."

Not quite finished, he turned back to them. "Look kids, we're not failures if we do our best, even if the world doesn't appear any better. We are to love, to give, to care, and to forgive, whether or not our efforts make a hostile world into a better place. The world may be facing some great new upheaval that might destroy our human effort, but those trees give me faith that there's something bigger than trees or man. If you two show the same determination that those trees do, it will work out all right." He paused, "I'm sorry, I didn't mean to be preachy. It's In my nature, I guess." He reached down and picked up his fly rod. "Why don't I try wetting a hook? Come on Beau."

CHAPTER 10

Noah woke up early. It was the day of the Fairview Fishing Frenzy and he didn't want to miss a minute. He and George made plans and had already paid the $2.00 entry fee. The main prize was a $100 Savings Bond and fishermen came from all around to compete. The rules stipulated only artificial bait could be used, and George had spent hours tying "special flies."

Mary and Thelma made them a big breakfast. George carried a thermos of coffee, along with some extra biscuits with bacon tucked into them so they wouldn't have to stop for lunch.

Joseph Hartley was in charge of the contest and was waiting at the dock where a large crowd of fishermen had already arrived. George and Noah registered their attendance and then walked to where Mr. Hartley stood.

"Morning George, Noah," said Mr. Hartley nodding to both.

"Morning Joseph," answered George. "Nice day for fishing."

"Big crowd. Going to be tough to win," said Mr. Hartley.

"Yep, just going to have to fish long and hard," said George.

"Well, you got a good helper," Mr. Hartley said, nodding at Noah.

"All right everyone, gather' round. I'm going to explain the rules," said Mr. Hartley.

They all surrounded Mr. Hartley as he explained what they could and could not do. Noah was standing near the edge of the crowd when he felt a shove in his back. He turned and came face to face with a grinning Bogey Harris.

"Hi, Jew lover," Bogey said. "I'm gonna' win this contest," he said in a hushed tone.

Noah nodded, not wanting to provoke him.

"What do you think of that?" Bogey asked trying to press the point. He looked around. "Where's your Jew bitch girlfriend?" Noah continued to ignore him.

Ann was helping her uncle in the drugstore, again saying she didn't want to show Noah up by catching the biggest fish.

"Tell me," Bogey asked, "what's that Jew meat like? Bet its real sweet." He grabbed his crotch and licked his lips, "might want to try some of that for myself."

Noah had had enough. He punched Bogey as hard as he could in the chest, then turned and quickly moved away.

"Ow!" Bogey hollered. "You better run, boy! I'm sure gonna' enjoy your girlfriend. Umm, I can taste her now," Bogey said, laughing and smacking his lips.

Noah was still upset when he came back to where his grandfather stood.

"What's eating you?" George asked.

"Ah, nothing much, Bogey Harris is giving me a hard time." Noah said.

"Try to avoid him. Time will take care of it" George replied.

"Yeah, he said he was going to win this tournament. He seemed pretty sure of it." Noah said.

"Well the only way he'll win is to cheat. Better keep an eye on him. Let's get our gear and get to fishing." George said.

They headed to a special "hole" that George liked to fish. On the way George spoke to Noah.

"You know Noah I am so proud of you and enjoy your company so much. You make fishing and life in general, fun again." George said.

"Thanks, I enjoy being with you, too." Noah replied, then asked, "what about Dad, didn't he like to fish?"

"Your father is a good man but he never really liked it here and only went fishing to appease me. He couldn't wait to leave Fairview. We are different but you are more like me and I am thankful for that," he said reaching out and putting his arm around Noah's shoulder.

"Thank you, Lord." Noah said to himself.

Bogey watched the fishermen as they went about their sport, which he cared nothing about. He only cared about the money, and he had a plan to claim it. He waited until they were all concentrating on their fishing. He then walked around the lake and up the stream that came down the mountain, and spilled into the lake. About half a mile up the stream there was a hole where the water was deeper.

When Bogey came to the spot, he hesitated, looking around, making sure no one saw him. He walked over to the water and moved away some brush, exposing a string running down into the water. He pulled it up and out came a wire cage with eight large trout. He had caught them over several days using natural bait and traps, both illegal in the contest. He inspected them and after ascertaining they were in good shape, placed them back into the water.

Reaching into his shirt pocket, he took out a plug of tobacco, broke off a piece, spit up a wad of phlegm, and placed the tobacco in his mouth. Deciding to wait awhile before turning them in as his catch for the day, he went over and sat down, leaning up against a tree. He began to think of what he would do with the money he was about to win and was soon fast asleep.

He heard a noise and followed the stream down the mountain to investigate. Ordinarily, he would have avoided such commotion, but he was hungry and could not afford to be as cautious as was his normal nature. His earlier injury had made it impossible to catch the fleet footed four-legs that he preferred to prey upon.

As he worked his way down the stream, he stayed in the brush until he came upon a two-leg out by itself. As he crouched down and watched, he used his senses to check for danger. He watched as the two-leg sat down by a tree and fell asleep. He thought how easy these animals were to catch. They were slow, careless, and weak. Waiting until he was sure the two-leg was asleep, he then worked his way as close as he dared, gathering his energy to spring.

Noah and his grandfather fished hard and caught four trout that were good enough to qualify for third place. They received a trophy and a yellow ribbon. All day Noah kept looking for Bogey.

"Wonder where Bogey is?" he asked his grandfather.

"Guess the competition was harder than he thought," he responded.

"Yeah, I guess so," Noah replied, but something didn't seem quite right and that gave him an uneasy feeling.

The whole valley was in turmoil. The mangled, decomposed body of the fisherman had been located as well as the remains of Bogey Harris. The state game department sent in a biologist who determined it was the work of a cougar, not a bear. Joseph Hartley organized a hunting party to search out and kill the animal that was doing the killing. Johnny Roberts brought in his pack of hunting dogs and everyone met at Hartley's store to plan their search. They divided into three groups and fanned out across the mountain, following the usual game and hiking trails of the slope.

George and Sam volunteered to help, but insisted on going alone. They did not want to be around the mob that was assembling. The men had been drinking and they felt that guns and alcohol did not mix. Also, it seemed unlikely with all the noise and commotion the men and dogs were making, that the animal would still be around. Noah wanted to go, but over his objections, they both insisted he should stay back at the store with Ann.

He heard the noise of the two-legs and the barkers and began to move away from them, up the mountain. His hip was hurting and the noise was particularly irritating. He had been following the scent of another cougar, this one a young male. He had been planning on making sure it left his territory, but now that could wait. He knew that near the crest of the mountain was a large rock outcropping where he could secretly keep watch on what was happening below.

"You and Sam come go with us," Joseph Hartley said.

"No thanks. I think we'll take Blu and check that area over there," George said, patting Blu on his head and pointing away from the assembly spot in front of Hartley's store.

"You don't think they'll find it?" George asked Sam as they walked away.

"No sir, that cat is smart to be able to have survived this long. He'll be holed up somewhere, just watching and waiting. He'll know for sure where they are long before they find him," Sam said as they started up the mountain.

"What do you think makes an animal turn to killing men?" George asked.

"Don't know for sure, but I can tell you one thing, he don't kill for pleasure, or jealousy, or greed, like men do. He only kills to protect himself or his young, or because he's hungry. I'd bet this animal is either too old or too hurt to be able to hunt so he's pickin' on easy targets like that fisherman and poor Bogey," Sam continued.

They had been gone for about an hour, letting Blu work, trying to pick up a scent. Suddenly, they heard a gunshot, followed quickly by two more. They looked at each other.

"What do you think?" Sam asked.

"Don't know. Sounds like they might have found something after all. Better check it out," George said. Working their way back down the trail, they reached the bottom where a large crowd was milling around and congratulating each other.

"You guys missed all the fun," Hartley said.

"You got him?" George asked.

"You better believe it," Hartley said, pointing at the carcass lying behind him by the steps of the store.

Pushing their way through the crowd Sam and George walked over to view the carcass. It was like a circus with everyone trying to get their picture made with "the beast". George pulled out his pipe, filled it with tobacco, lit up, and studied the animal. Sam bent down and felt the body, pulling back the skin on its muzzle, exposing the teeth and gums.

"Hey." Came a voice.

They looked up to see Noah and Ann.

"That's some animal," Noah said, as he bent down to study it.

"I've never seen one, have you?" Ann asked Noah.

"Not in the wild, just in zoos. Who shot him?" Noah asked.

"Mr. Hartley and some of the men," George said.

"Well, I guess that's that. Everything ought to be okay now," Noah said.

"Yes, I guess so," George said, looking at Sam.

Ann and Noah headed back home, now that the excitement had died down.

"What do you think?" George asked Sam.

"Don't know. That isn't a full-grown cat, I can tell you that," Sam said.

"Yeah, I got kind of an uneasy feeling about it. I just don't see that animal having the will or the ability to do what they say it did." George said. He hesitated, and then looked at Sam. "I hope I'm wrong." George said, sounding worried.

"Yes sir, I do too, Dr. George." Sam said.

Hearing the noise of the thunder sticks, he had become agitated. Suddenly, the noise seemed to move away from him back down the hill towards the two-legs lair. Relieved, he relaxed and enjoyed the warmth of the sun on his damaged hip. He decided to wait a while before leaving the rock outcrop.

Noah, along with Ann and his Grandfather, attended the funeral of Bogey Harris. There were only a handful of people at the simple graveside service. For the first time Noah saw Bogey's father, standing beside the coffin, looking lost and, Noah thought, afraid.

As the three of them left the cemetery, his grandfather told Noah and Ann how proud he was of them for putting differences aside and attending the service of their former nemesis.

"It shows a lot of character for you two to make an effort to attend the funeral of someone like that," George said.

"I don't think Bogey could help it," Noah mused. "I don't know how I would have turned out if the circumstances had been reversed. I just hope he's at peace now that he's with God."

His grandfather put his arm around him, "Well said, but I don't think you have it in you to be like that, no matter what the circumstances."

Later that evening, as Noah and Ann walked hand and hand down to Riverside Park, he reminisced about spending hours as a child playing on the playground equipment. Now he simply enjoyed the park for its beauty. It was built on a point of land that jutted out into the lake, so that it was surrounded by water on three sides. There were maples, ponderosa pine, oaks, and huge stands of mountain laurel, all in a setting of lush mountain grasses studded with granite rocks, left strewn about from the last ice age.

He and Ann sat on the swings and began to slowly move back and forth.

"I sure am glad they got that cougar. I'll feel a lot safer when we go walking," Noah said.

"Me too. I feel sorry for that poor fisherman and Bogey but I am glad they got the cougar. I wonder if Bogey ever realized that Jesus was a Jew who preached love and forgiveness. I hope he's found it." Ann said.

Noah reached over and squeezed her hand, wondering what he ever did to deserve someone like her.

She was quiet for a moment, and then exclaimed, "I've never seen so many fireflies."

"There's always a lot here, because of all the plants and the moisture. My friend David and I used to catch them back home and smear their bodies on our clothes and skin so we would glow." Noah said.

"Oh, that's cruel and nasty," Ann protested.

"I was a kid! I wouldn't do it now," he answered defensively.

"I think there are almost as many fireflies as there are stars," she said, looking up at the sky. "Do you think there's life up there?" She asked.

"I don't know, maybe." He said.

"I hope if there is, they do a better job of living together than we do." She replied.

"I wouldn't count on it. They probably would be just like us, except they might be more advanced and better able to destroy each other." He said.

"I hope not, I hope they've learned to live together in peace." She sighed.

"Maybe so." He said.

He got up, pulled her from the swing and took her in his arms, giving her a kiss.

"I love you my worrying little Earthling." He said, holding her tight and smiling.

"Umm, I don't know if anyone's up there, but I'm glad to be here on Earth with you," she said, kissing him back.

CHAPTER 11

Noah awoke to another beautiful morning, one of those perfect high mountain days when the sky is clear azure blue and the meadows are a riot of color, waving in the gentle breeze.

"Morning Thelma," he said groggily, entering the kitchen.

"Good morning, Noah. Are you hungry?" She asked.

"Yes, ma'am," Noah replied.

"Well, sit down. Your Grandfather went to Mr. Hartley's store to talk to some fishermen about making flies, and your grandmother took some chicken soup over to Mrs. Wilson. Seems she has a cold and your grandmother thought it would make her feel better." Thelma said.

Thelma fried him an egg, along with some bacon and toast.

"Sure was something about that big cat they got. That cat really scared me." She said with a shudder.

"Yeah, did you see it?" he asked.

"No, I'd just as soon stay away," she said.

"Sam said he might make you a coat out of it," he said, goading her, with a big grin on his face.

Thelma looked at him, puzzled for a moment, and then realized he was kidding. She picked up a towel and popped him with it.

"Ow," he said, laughing.

"That'll teach you to try and fool me." Thelma laughed.

Noah had noticed the playfulness between Thelma and Sam and wanted to ask her how they were getting along, but decided it was not the right time.

"Boy, it's a beautiful day," Noah said. Leaning back and folding his arms behind his head.

"It certainly is," she agreed. "The Lord did a good job."

"I think I'll see if Ann would like to go on a picnic." Noah said.

"That would be a good idea, especially now that they killed that cat," Thelma said.

Noah called Ann, and she agreed to go along and said she would bring some of her Aunt's pie. Thelma helped him pack a picnic basket, which he took and headed for Ann's.

"Where's Noah?" George asked Thelma when he returned home later that morning.

"He and Ann went on a picnic," Thelma said.

"Where'd they go?" George asked with a note of concern.

Thelma could tell he was upset. "I don't know. Is something wrong?" she asked.

"No, probably not." He waited a minute then added, "I'm going over to Sam's."

When Sam saw George, he could tell he was upset about something.

"What's wrong?" Sam asked.

"Probably nothing," George said. He told Sam about the picnic.

"I just have an uneasy feeling about the kids going off. I wish I knew for sure that the cougar they killed was the right one." George said.

"Yeah, me too," Sam said. "What do you want to do?"

"I don't know. I hate for the kids to think I'm spying on them, but this feeling just won't go away." George said.

"Do you know where they went?" Sam asked.

"Not for sure, but I bet they went up to that rock outcropping. It's Noah's favorite place." George said.

"I'll tell you what. I'll get my gun and Blu and we'll go out looking for them. If we see them, we'll say we're out hunting and didn't know they were there." Sam said.

"Good idea. Thanks, Sam," George said.

"You look beautiful today," Noah said when he saw Ann.

"Thank you, kind sir. I have some pie and I brought a blanket." Ann said smiling up at Noah.

"You kids enjoy yourselves, but be careful," said Mrs. Zimmerman, then added, "Are you taking Beau?"

"No ma'am, he won't leave the food alone," Noah said, but in truth they wanted to be alone.

Noah took Ann's hand, and they started toward the mountain.

"Oh, Noah, it is such a pretty day." Ann said with a smile.

"Yeah and you make it even prettier." Noah said.

"You sure know how to get a girl's attention," she said, giving him a quick kiss on the cheek.

It took almost an hour to reach the rock outcropping. They were hot and tired, and decided to spread the blanket out and rest a few minutes before they ate. He awoke, amazed that 'a few minutes' had turned into almost an hour. Noah turned to Ann, studying her, taking in her quiet, natural beauty with reverent awe. "Hey," he said softly as she stirred.

"Hey yourself," she replied, smiling.

"I love you," he said.

"When?" she asked, looking at him.

"What do you mean?" He asked puzzled.

"When did you first know you were in love with me?" She replied.

He hesitated for a moment, "It was when you caught that fish. Watching you try so hard to please Granddad and me." He said.

She smiled and said, "I think for me, it was when your mother started to question me. You realized it was making me uncomfortable and suggested we go for a walk. Oh Noah," she cried, kissing him with all of the ardor that she possessed. "I love you so very, very much," she said. "I don't want to go back. I wish the next few weeks would last forever."

"Marry me and stay here with me." He said, taking her into his arms.

"I can't, not now. I have to go back, but I will return. I don't want to be without you. I want to be with you forever." Ann said, pulling back and looking into his eyes.

"Me, too, and a day," he said, as he again took her in his arms.

Once again, the world around them dissolved away and only the passion of the moment remained.

He had been roaming away from the rock looking for food, still cautious about going too close to the area where the two- legs made their dens. He was returning to get a better view when he picked up their scent. Slowly he circled, until he worked his way to the ledge and could see all around him. There below he could clearly see them now. He studied them, relieved there was no barker with them. As he watched, he was puzzled as they began putting on their skins.

Ann moved out of Noah's embrace and said, "Let's get dressed. I got chilly lying in the shade."

"Yeah, me too, let's eat, I'm starved." Noah said.

"You men, exercise always makes you hungry," she said, laughing.

As he pulled on his jeans and shirt, he watched her getting dressed. She ran her fingers through her hair. He knew that he could never quit loving her. It seemed he had known her forever and that he always would.

He watched closely as they sat down and brought out food. The smell was overpowering, and he could no longer control his hunger. His hip had never healed right and he could not run after the fast game he was used to. He had to eat and decided not to wait any longer. If he had been in better shape and not weakened from hunger, he might have pounced from the ledge, but he knew he had to use a different tactic. He moved off the ledge and worked around the base, keeping himself hidden in the brush. He was now as close as he could get. He crouched to a springing position, tensed his muscles and, having decided to attack the larger two-leg first, pounced.

"No!" Ann screamed.

Noah turned just as the cougar struck him, its claws raking into his leg. The force of the blow knocked Noah over. His head struck a rock and filled with a thousand explosions of light as he lost consciousness.

Ann screamed again. The cougar turned towards her. For a moment she stood, transfixed. She started to run and then realized there was no way she could outrun it. She quickly bent down and picked up a rock, throwing it at the creature. It gave out a howl as it hit on his side. Infuriated, he began to circle her. She threw another rock, this time hitting his bad hip. He screeched in pain and leapt at her. Suddenly, Blu burst from the bushes and attacked the cougar, causing it to momentarily lose its concentration. Blu barked and attacked the animal's rear. The cougar turned and swatted at Blu, connecting with a powerful swipe of its paw, sending him sprawling. The cougar was enraged, mad with pain, and beyond its normal ability to reason. Ann backed away and was now standing against the rock, waving a small limb she had picked up. The cougar snarled and crouched, then released its compacted muscles, springing at Ann.

Once more Ann screamed, swinging the tree branch. Suddenly there was a shot and the cougar shuddered and fell just short of her. Ann stood, shaking and sobbing, watching as George and Sam moved into the clearing.

"You okay?" George asked.

Ann couldn't speak. She just shivered and nodded her head in affirmation. George reached out and removed the branch that Ann still clutched in her hand and then hurried over to Noah where he bent down, feeling for a pulse.

"He's alive," he said to Ann. Turning him over, he saw the blood on the back of his head where he had hit the rock. Then he examined the lacerations on his leg where the claws had bloodied him.

"I think he'll be okay but he may have a concussion. How's Blu?" George asked, turning to Sam.

"Believe he's going to be okay," Sam said, as he stroked his dog's head.

George got up and walked over to the carcass of the cougar, nudging it to make sure it was dead.

"Look at that," he said, pointing to the cougar's injured flank, "No wonder he had to turn man killer." He turned to Ann.

"Can you walk?" He asked.

"Ye...yes" she finally replied.

"Well, let's try and get everyone back to town. We need to treat Noah and Blu." He studied Ann for a moment, then put his arm around her, "You did really well. I am so glad you came through."

They quickly made a litter out of saplings and their coats, placed Noah and Blu on it, and started down the mountain. They would send a party to retrieve the Cougars carcass.

CHAPTER 12

"Oh, my Lord, what happened?" Thelma gasped as they brought Noah into the house.

"Thelma, please, go get Mary," George said. When they returned, George quickly explained what happened and assured them that Noah would be all right. Sam put his arm around Thelma to comfort her.

"We need to clean the wounds and keep him off that leg. He has a concussion so don't let him fall asleep until I say it's okay," George said.

Sam laid Noah on the bed and Mary and Thelma took charge of getting him cleaned up.

"You all go on. Get out of here. Thelma and I'll take care of him," Mary said, as she shooed everyone out the door.

Sam, George, and Ann all went into the living room and sat down.

"He will be all right, won't he?" Ann asked anxiously, as all three went into the living room and sat down.

"Yes. We just need to watch him and make sure we keep his leg wound clean. Don't want any infection." George said.

"I'll stay with him," Ann said.

"I thought you might. Just make sure to check him for fever and check that his pupils don't become dilated," George said. "If any of those things happen, get me right away."

Ann went home to clean up and change clothes. The word of the attack had already spread throughout town. When she told her aunt she was going to stay at the Johnson's to help take care of Noah, her aunt protested but, after Ann explained the situation, and seeing how adamant she was, her aunt relented and let Ann go back to Noah.

"How is he?" Ann asked anxiously upon her return.

"He's fine, go on in. There is no sign of a concussion so I gave him a sedative to help him sleep and I treated and bandaged his leg. He'll feel a lot better when he wakes up and sees you here." George said.

Ann tiptoed into the room and over to the bed where Noah lay, with Thelma sitting next to him, watching. Ann touched his face, then leaned down and gave him a kiss on his cheek.

"Here, Miss Ann," Thelma said, offering up her chair.

"Thanks Thelma. Where's Sam?" Ann asked.

"He went home to take care of Blu." Thelma replied.

"Oh!" exclaimed Ann, "I forgot about Blu. Is he all right?"

"Yes ma'am, he's going to be fine," Thelma said, studying Ann. "And so is Mr. Noah," she said, putting her arm around Ann's shoulder.

"Thanks," Ann said, patting Thelma's arm. "Thanks." she repeated. After a moment of quiet reflection Ann broke the silence.

"How about you and Sam? How are you two getting along? Are you seeing him a lot? Has he said he cares about you?" Ann asked.

"Lord Miss Ann, you need to slow down!" Thelma said, laughing. "Sam and me, we've been seeing each other pretty regular." She hesitated, looking around. "Can you keep a secret?"

Ann nodded.

"Sam's asked me to marry him." Thelma said.

"Oh, Thelma, I'm so glad! What did you say?" Ann asked anxiously.

Thelma grinned, "I made him sweat a little then said yes."

Ann squealed and hugged her. "When?"

"Just the other day," Thelma replied.

"No silly, I mean when will you get married." Ann asked.

"We thought we'd wait till Noah's parents come back." She said.

"That's less than a month from now, and then I'll have to leave shortly after that" Ann said.

"What about you and Mr. Noah?" Not speaking, Ann shrugged her shoulders. "Don't you love him?" Thelma asked.

"Yes, oh yes, Thelma, with all my heart." Ann said wishfully.

"Then why not marry him and stay?" Thelma asked.

"It's not that simple." Ann answered with a shrug.

"Child, I'm not real smart, but I know that what matters most above all else in this world is love. If we just would learn to love and let ourselves be loved, this old world would be a lot better place. I know Noah loves you and you love him. Nothing else really matters." Thelma said.

"I wish it were enough," Ann said.

"It is. Believe me, Miss Ann, it is." Thelma said.

Ann spent the rest of the day sitting by Noah's bedside while George and Mary changed his bandages and Thelma made them all sandwiches. Noah slept as a result of his ordeal and the sedative George had given him. George checked Noah's temperature, pulse, and blood pressure, and pronouncing them normal, and then announced that there was still no sign of a concussion. Ann insisted on staying the night and George brought her a cup of cocoa.

"I thought you might like this," he said, handing the cocoa to her.

"Thanks. Are you sure he's okay?" Ann asked.

"Don't worry. He's going to be just fine. He'll just be a little sore for a few days." He hesitated a moment, studying her. "It's not any of my business, but I have been hoping that you and Noah would remain together. You've been a Godsend to him, and to us. Noah needs direction in his life. He's a smart young man, but he needs to have something to anchor him. I think you are what he needs more than anything in his life." He put his hand on her shoulder, patted her arm and kissed her forehead.

"Whatever happens between you and Noah, I want you to know that we all are glad you came into his life and ours." George said.

"Thank you. I am too," she said, fighting to hold back her tears.

Ann spent the night in the old overstuffed chair by the window. She thought about what Thelma and George had said and realized it all made sense. Finally, she fell asleep as the events of the day caught up, and she did not awaken until the sunlight spilled through the window, hitting her face. She stretched gingerly and then sat up, quickly looking at Noah, only to find him looking back at her.

"Good morning sleepy head," he said.

"How are you?" Ann asked anxiously.

"I'm fine. At least I will be when I find whoever came into the room and messed in my mouth." Noah said with a grimace.

"Noah!" She admonished. "I'm being serious. How are you feeling?"

"I'm okay, really, just a little sore." He reached out and took her hand. "Thanks for being here, for caring about me." He held her hand and smiled.

"I love you." She replied gazing into his eyes and stroking his head.

"Forever?" He asked smiling.

"And a day," she said bending over and hugging him. She pulled back quickly. "I didn't hurt you, did I?" Ann asked.

"No, you goose, you make me feel better." He suddenly became somber and said in a pensive voice, "I would feel a lot better if you would agree to marry me."

She was stunned for a moment as his request sank in, then gushed out, "Yes, oh yes."

He sat up quickly, wincing, "Did you just say yes?" He asked incredulously.

"Yes, my love, yes, I'll marry you." She said smiling.

"What.... When?" He asked elated by her answer.

"Now," she exclaimed.

"But what about all of your fears?" He asked.

"My darling, all this made me realize that my main fear is not having you in my life." She said, and then carefully hugged him.

Ann called out for George and Mary, who came running into the room.

"Is he okay?" George asked anxiously.

They were surprised to see the two of them holding hands and smiling.

"You two look like the cat that ate the canary," George said. "How do you feel?" He asked Noah.

"Fine, I'm a little sore. Ann and I have something to tell you; we've decided to get
married." Noah said with a smile.

"Congratulations, that's the best medicine in the world. We've been praying it would work out. You two are made for each other," George said. He carefully shook Noah's hand and gave Ann a hug.

"Thank you, for helping me realize what I needed to do," Ann whispered to George.

Mary came over and hugged Ann. "I'm so glad for you both. You already seem like one of the family." She looked at Noah, "I hope you know how lucky you are."

"Yes ma'am, I do." Noah responded.

Thelma was ecstatic when Ann told her. They laughed, cried, and danced around.

"Oh, Miss Ann, I'm so excited. Have you set a date? You could have it at the same time Sam and I do." Thelma said.

"We have to tell Noah's parents, and then decide where and when. Thelma, I am excited, but I'm scared too. I just hope I'm doing the right thing." Ann said.

"Honey, that's natural. There hasn't been a bride yet who wasn't scared before the wedding. The very fact that you worry about it means you are being realistic and not blind. It'll work out just fine," she said, putting her arms around Ann and hugging her.

Ann decided to run over to her aunt and uncle's house to tell them the news.

"You what! Have you lost your mind?" Her uncle said proclaiming the folly of such a union.

"Now Ira, let her talk," replied her aunt.

"I love him and I can't imagine life without him," Ann said.

"You're too young, and besides that, he's not Jewish," her uncle responded.

"You two got married when Aunt Ruth was just sixteen and he may not be Jewish, but he's not prejudiced either. He's very accepting, and kind, and loving and…"

Her aunt put her arm around her. "It's okay Honey, you obviously love him and I doubt anything we say is going to change that. Have you told your parents?"

"No Ma'am. I thought I would write them a letter. I think it would be better than a telegram." Ann replied.

"Nonsense, we'll call them," her aunt said.

Her aunt glanced toward her husband, giving him a warning look, knowing he might protest the cost. They placed the call, and an hour later the operator called back to say she had them on the line. Ann talked, with occasional input from her aunt, for a half hour explaining the situation. At first her parents were shocked and protested but gradually relented after her Aunt got on the line and explained what a good young man Noah was and how he wanted to be a doctor and come back to Fairview to practice.

"You what!" Louise shouted into the phone. "Noah, have you lost your mind? You can't do that, you're only twenty. You don't have a job, or a place to live. You have your whole life before you, you…."

"Mother, listen, in a few weeks I'll be twenty-one. I love Ann and she loves me. I know there are a lot of problems but we'll have a lifetime to work them out. We thought we would get married when you come up. It's the same time that Thelma and Sam are, getting married." Noah said.

"Thelma and Sam; they're getting married too?" His mother asked incredulously.

"Yes, like I said. We're going to make it a double wedding," Noah replied. "Be sure and tell David and see if he can come," he added.

Louise did not want to talk anymore, so she said goodbye and hung up. The first thing she did was to call Arthur at the store and tell him.

"Can you believe it?" she asked, still in shock from the call.

"They seem very much in love." Arthur replied.

"It doesn't surprise me about Thelma and Sam. She would do anything to keep from coming back, and after all I have done for her." Louise said.

"My dear, I think you have that backwards. Besides, last time I checked, slavery has ended." Arthur said.

"But what about Noah?" she continued, ignoring his comment. "How will they live? Where will they live? What will he do? What about the fact that she's Jewish?" she asked, unable to mask her concern.

"Louise, Noah can work in the store. We could fix up that space over the garage or they could have Noah's room. As for Ann being Jewish, well, they will have to work that out, and I'm sure they can." Arthur said.

"You mean you're for this?" Louise asked.

"It's not up to me," he paused, "or you. It is their life and their future." He said.

The next morning Ann saw Mary working in her garden and decided to stop and visit with her. As Ann approached, Mary looked up.

"Good morning Ann." Mary said, waving.

"Good morning, Mrs. Johnson. Are you planting?" Asked Ann.

"My dear, you're practically one of the family. Please call me Mary. I'm working the soil, getting it ready for planting. I have to condition it by adding organic matter and manure, and then I work it in with a spade. It keeps the soil loose and fertile."

"Can I try?" Ann asked.

"Sure, let me show you how." Mary said.

Mary gave her a spade and a pair of gloves, and began to show her how to turn the soil and add the mulch and manure. As they worked, Mary studied Ann. When she noticed her digging in the same spot over and over Mary asked, "Is something troubling you child?"

"Yes ma'am, uh, Mary." Ann said.

"Do you want to talk about it?" Mary asked.

Ann looked at her then and said, "I guess I'm worried. I'm worried about the wedding. I love Noah, but I'm not sure that's enough. When you married Dr. Johnson were you certain?" Ann asked.

"Heavens child, I almost didn't marry him!" Mary said with a chuckle.

Ann looked shocked, "But you both seem so happy."

"We are. But at the time, I had doubts. I had known George for several years and we were friends, but I never thought of him in a romantic sense. He was just good old George, someone to go to the movies with or to go get a malt." Mary said.

Ann looked at her quizzically, "What happened?" She asked.

"I started going out with other boys. I didn't realize it at the time, but I hurt George because he had fallen in love with me. I wanted more. I wanted to be swept off my feet by some Prince Charming, or so I thought. I wanted the big cities and bright lights." She hesitated and looked at Ann. "I'm afraid Louise is a lot like I was then. Anyway, I dated four or five boys, but it always seemed like something was missing until one day it dawned on me – I loved George. I hadn't wanted to admit it, because it wasn't what I thought I needed. I thought I wanted a roaring fire, but I finally settled for a constant flame, one that wouldn't be all consuming and burn itself out, but one that would burn steadily through all of life's storms. I haven't regretted it in all these years!" Mary explaimed.

Mary reached over and put her arm around Ann. "You see, it's like this soil. It's plain and barren until we add mulch and fertilizer, plant the seeds, and water and care for them. Then over a period of time something beautiful happens." She studied Ann for a moment. "It'll work out, Honey. Just give it a lot of love and…," she laughed, "a good dose of manure!"

CHAPTER 13

The wedding was three weeks away, and it seemed time had slowed to a crawl. Ann, along with Thelma, Ruth, and Mary, had been making plans for the double wedding ceremony. Ann and Noah realized that their birthdays were just ten days apart, so they decided to have a joint birthday and engagement party. Everyone in Fairview was invited to the Pavilion at Riverside Park. Joseph Hartley brought his guitar, enlisting Lucy Krebs to play the piano, and recruited several other musicians to join them. Each family signed up to bring a covered dish, with the Rotary Club volunteering to donate and cook the meat for the barbecue. The Watering Hole Bar supplied the beer and Ira Zimmerman gave the soft drinks and the ingredients for the ice cream. The women spent the morning decorating, blowing up balloons, stringing crepe paper and Japanese lanterns. All in all, it would be a big and very festive occasion. Noah was surprised when he realized that he was sorry his parents would not be there, since they were waiting for the wedding in three weeks. They had sent a present that he was anxious to open.

George got up and stood on the gazebo to make his announcements.

"I want to welcome each of you to the birthday party for Noah and Ann. Since their birthdays are only ten days apart, they decided to celebrate together. Later, I want to make an announcement about their future, but for now, just enjoy all the food and drink that each of you was kind enough to bring. I especially want to thank the Rotary Club for providing and cooking the meat. Noah and Ann are blessed to have loving friends like all of you." George said.

Everyone moved to the tables, and after the blessing was given, they began to eat.

"Boy, I don't know when I've eaten so much," Noah said, rubbing his stomach.

"Yeah, I need side boards on my plate," Sam said.

"No one made you two eat like a couple of starving mules. Isn't that right honey?" Thelma said, putting her arm around Ann, who shook her head in affirmation.

"Lord, I'm going to have to sew gussets in your pants," Thelma said to Sam with a laugh.

George motioned to Ann and Noah to join him at the gazebo. "If you two are through eating you might want to open your presents."

Noah and Ann went into the gazebo where a table was set up to hold the gifts. They began to open them, thanking each one who brought something. Sam gave Noah a carving of a cougar and Ann a carving of a dog that looked remarkably like Beau. Thelma gave Ann a box Sam had carved and in which she had put copies of her recipes. Noah received a box of her special cookies and a shirt she had sewn. George gave Noah a medical dictionary and Ann a painting of the lake. Mary gave one of her quilts to them both. The Zimmerman's gave them each twenty dollars. Noah could not wait any longer to open the gift from his parents. Tearing into it, he found a car key. Puzzled, he read the attached note in his father's handwriting.

> Noah,
> Wish we could be there with you and Ann, but we will see you in three weeks for the wedding. Enclosed are the keys to the Chevy. We bought a new one and are giving you the old one so you and Ann will have transportation. It will be waiting for you when you come home.
> Happy birthday, Dad, Mom and Michael
>
> P.S. Watch out for the chickens.

Noah let out a loud whoop as he grabbed Ann and started dancing around, letting his excitement overflow. He showed the letter to Ann.

"Sweetheart, that's great! We'll have a car, and maybe you can teach me to drive. But what is that post script about chickens?" She asked.

Noah laughed, "When I first started learning to drive Dad would take me out on country roads to practice. One time we were coming over a hill and below us was a flock of chickens out on the road. I went to put on the brakes, but in my anxiety I hit the foot feed instead. We plowed right through those chickens. Feathers, blood, and guts covered the car. When we got home, Dad made me spend an hour cleaning off the car."

Ann laughed and then gave him her present. He opened it and pulled out a leather lanyard to which was attached one of the Cougar's claws.

"Hey, this is great. Thanks sweetheart," he said, placing it around his neck.

"It took that cougar to make me realize that no matter what else happens, you are the most important thing in my life. Noah, I simply could not face a world without you." Ann said, gazing up at him.

He wanted to kiss her but refrained with everyone watching.

"Now for yours." He handed her the present and stepped back to watch as she opened it pulling it from the box, Ann stared at it and then broke down with a sob.

"Oh, Noah it's beautiful," she said holding up the silver medallion on a silver chain with two entwined hearts, one labeled Noah, the other Ann. On the back it read, 'Forever and a day'. "I love you so," Ann whispered through tears of happiness.

Everyone clapped as he took her into his arms and throwing caution to the wind, kissed her. "I love you, too, forever and a day." Noah said smiling at her.

Later that afternoon, after everyone had finished the cake and ice cream, George got up to make his announcement.

"Most of you know that Sam and Thelma are getting married in three weeks, but some of you may not know that my grandson, Noah, and his fiancée, Ann, will be joining them. We'll have a double wedding and everyone is invited." George said.

There were cheers of "Congratulations" and "Best wishes!" George pushed Sam and Noah, over their protests, up onto the stage to say a few words.

"I don't know what to say except, I love her and I don't deserve her," Sam said, looking at Thelma. "And I'll take good care of her from now on."

Everyone applauded. There were calls of, "You sure don't!" and, "Remember that!" all given with hoots of laughter.

It was Noah's turn. He hesitated, and then began. "I've always loved these mountains and this town, this place, and especially each of you. But now, I have someone to share that love with and I have to be the luckiest guy alive." He reached out and pulled Ann close to him, looking into her, big, and deep, tear-filled eyes. He said softly, "I'm the luckiest man that ever lived, on this planet or any other."

CHAPTER 14

The next few days were some of the most enjoyable Noah had ever spent. Ann was happy and smiling. For the first time, she seemed to have forgotten all about the world outside and thought only of their world. He prayed that she would stay that way. Each day that passed made him realize even more how much he loved her. For the first time, they felt free to display their affection in public. Noah was enjoying being able to hug and kiss Ann without sneaking around.

One morning he was lying in bed reminiscing about all this, when his grandmother knocked on the door.

"Noah," Mary said.

"Yes?" he answered.

"Ann's here," she said.

"What?" he asked.

"She's upset. You need to come out." Mary said.

"What's the matter?" He asked, Mary.

"I don't know, she wouldn't say, just hurry." Mary said.

"Ok, I'll be right there," he said.

He hurried to put on his clothes and went out to meet her. She was standing on the porch. He could hear her sobbing from inside the house. He put his arms around her, holding her against his chest, feeling her shake with each wave of tears.

"What's the matter sweetheart?" Noah asked.

She didn't answer, only pulling him tighter.

"Ann, darling, what's wrong? Please tell me," Noah asked again, alarmed by her distress.

She reached into her pocket and handed him a wrinkled sheet of paper. He recognized that it was a telegram, which he opened and read. It was from her mother, informing her that her father had died suddenly of a heart attack, and begging Ann to come home at once.

"Oh, darling, I'm so sorry," he said, continuing to hold her, as he asked, "What are we going to do?"

"I have to go. I don't want to leave you Noah, but my mother and sister need me." She began to cry again, "Oh Noah, help me. Please tell me what to do." Ann said pleadingly.

He led her over to the porch swing where they sat down. He put his arm back around her and pulled her to his shoulder.

"Darling I'm so sorry about your father and I know your mother needs you. I don't want to be selfish about it," he said, suddenly feeling much older than twenty-one. "Damn it, this isn't fair", he thought.

"But what about the wedding?" Ann asked.

He thought for a few moments and then said, "Let's just move it up. We'll get married right away, there's no reason why we have to wait." He said.

"What about your family?" She asked.

"They'll understand. Maybe we can do it again when we come back." He said.

"We?" She asked.

"Yes, I'm going with you. I can help and we will be in Paris." He said.

"No, Noah. I know you would go and I appreciate it. But you need to stay here and get enrolled in medical school and make arrangements for us to have a place to live when I return." He started to protest, but she stopped him. "We don't need to spend the extra money. We'll need it later. Besides, with you here, I can concentrate on what I need to do and I'll have added incentive to get things taken care of a lot quicker." She said, grasping his hand.

"What about your fears?" He asked.

"I'll be back before anything can happen," She said.

He got up quickly, pulling her up with him.

"Yeah, you're right. I don't like it, but it does make sense. Come on; let's go talk to my grandparents, and your aunt and uncle, so we can make the arrangements. You need to let your mother know." He kissed her lips, tasting the salt from her tears.

George and Mary were sad about Ann's father, but were thrilled about the wedding. "We're so sorry about your father. I know it was a terrible decision to have to make, but I think you made the right one." George said.

"I hope so," Noah thought, still having reservations about not going.

"I'm so happy that you decided to go ahead with the wedding," Mary said, hugging Ann. Suddenly she pulled away with a worried look. "What about your gown," she asked?

"I won't have time to make one. I'll just have to make do with what I have," Ann said.

"Nonsense," Mary said, "come with me." She led Ann into the bedroom and over to a trunk at the end of the bed. Opening it, she reached in and brought out a package, which she undid and held up its contents: her own wedding gown.

"It's beautiful," Ann said breathlessly.

"I want you to wear it," Mary said.

"Oh, I couldn't!" Ann said excited.

"Don't be silly. I want you to have it. It brought me a wonderful love and I'll never need it again. I know it will do the same for you," Mary said.

"You're too nice to me. I love you, all of you, so very much," Ann said her eyes full of tears.

Mary hugged her. "We all love you too, now come on, let's go tell the men."

Everything was worked out. They would get married in two days and then Noah would drive them in George's car to the city. They would spend their honeymoon at the hotel that night, then Ann would catch the train the next morning and travel to New York, then by ship, on to Paris.

Ann telegraphed her mother letting her know the plans and then spent the rest of the day packing, saying goodbye, and finalizing her travel arrangements. Noah secured the Justice of the Peace, Frank Haywood, to perform the wedding. Ira would give Ann away, and Sam was to be Noah's best man, with Thelma the bride's maid. Noah's parents had planned on bringing the ring, one that had been Louise's mother's, but since they wouldn't be there on time, George bought each of them a plain gold band to use.

When Noah called his parents Louise was upset, saying it was an "omen" and "this marriage wasn't meant to be." Arthur finally calmed her down and explained to her at least now she wouldn't have to worry about what to wear. Michael was excited because he wouldn't have to wear a suit and be in the wedding.

Noah asked if they had told David he was getting married and to let him know about the change of plans. His father said David was not going to be able to come, since he had just started a new job. Noah thought it curious that this upset him more than his parents not being there.

The next day Ann came over. She had finished packing, and since everything had been arranged, she suggested they visit their special place one last time before she left.

"That's a great idea, but I don't like it when you say 'last'." Noah said.

"Okay, silly, until I return, never to leave again." Ann said giving him a hug.

The overcast sky did nothing to diminish the giddiness they felt as they made their way up the mountain. The wildflowers were in full bloom and the air was infused with their fragrance. Bees and butterflies fluttered all around on their single-minded purpose of gathering the riches before them.

"God, I love the beauty here." Noah said in a prayerful manner.

"I can't get over the wonderful fragrance the flowers create," Ann said, taking a deep breath. "It's as if nature created its own Perfume."

When they arrived, they sat down at the spot where they had first met.

"Darling, I just had to be with you here, once more, before I leave. I'll carry the thought of this place and you in my heart. It will make our time apart a little easier to bear," Ann said.

"This place always had special meaning for me. But without you, it's nothing. From now on, it will always be our place. I can't picture it without you." He took her in his arms, kissing her deeply.

"Forever," she whispered.

"And a day," he said, kissing her once more.

There was a clap of thunder.

"Sounds like a vote of approval," Noah said with a laugh. "I think we better start back."

They had only gone part way when the rain began.

"There's an old abandoned cabin just a little way off the trail," Noah said. "These afternoon mountain storms don't last long. We can wait it out there."

They covered their heads with the parkas they were wearing and ran the few hundred yards to the cabin. The dilapidated cabin had a sagging roof at one end and all the glass gone from the windows. The front door lay on the ground, but the fireplace chimney was still standing.

"There's a dry place over by the fireplace. I'll see if there are any matches around and build a small fire. The chimney is probably stopped up but there's certainly enough ventilation so we won't suffocate." Noah said.

He looked around and found a jar with matches in it. He tore down an abandoned bird nest and some old newspaper that had been placed on the wall for insulation and added pieces of old boards. Soon he had a small fire going.

"There, that makes it feel like home." He said, with a laugh, and then put his arms around Ann. "You know, I wonder what happened to the people who lived here, what lives they lived, what happiness and sorrows they knew. It's sort of like as long as it stands, this place is a monument to their lives."

Ann said nothing but reached up and kissed him. They sat wrapped in each other's arms next to the small fire.

That evening, after returning from their hike, Noah went over to the Zimmerman's for dinner. Mary had cut some of her roses and other flowers to fashion a bouquet for Ann to carry and she used some of the extras to make an arrangement for Noah to take with him. He knocked on their door, and when Mrs. Zimmerman answered, he handed her the flowers.

"Hello Noah," she said, "Oh, thank you. My, aren't these pretty! Come on in son. Ann's in the kitchen."

She led Noah to the back where Ann was icing a cake. Ann looked up and Noah's heart skipped when he saw her smiling once again. She put down the knife she was using and ran to hug him. He started to speak, but she shook her head no and whispered. "Don't say anything, just hold me." Finally, she pulled back and looked at him, "Just think, this is the last night we will spend as two separate people. Tomorrow we will become one spirit," she said, smiling.

"And for every tomorrow afterwards," Noah answered.

Ira walked in. "All right you two lovebirds, are we going to eat, or what?"

They moved to the table and Ruth and Ann brought in the meal. Noah had not known what to expect. He had entertained visions of strange looking and tasting foods. He was both relieved, and a little disappointed, when he was served fried chicken, which he made up his mind to eat and green beans, mashed potatoes, and homemade bread.

Ira looked at Noah "We give a prayer called the Hamastzi, which is sung before meals where there is bread," Ira said. Noah repeated the name and Ira corrected him.

Ira began to sing:

> Hamastzi lechem min ha'aretz
> We give thanks to God for bread
> Our voices rise in song together
> As our joyful prayer is said:
> Baruch atah adonai,
> Elohaynu melech ha'olam
> Hamatzi lechem min ha'aretz

As Ira sang, Noah thought it interesting and certainly far different from anything he had ever known. They ate and talked about the wedding, the weather, the trip, Ann's mother, and her sister. Finally, Ira asked Noah, "What do you know about Judaism?"

"Not much." Noah said.

"Now Ira, we don't have to discuss that now." Ruth said.

"No, it's all right. I would like to learn more." Noah said.

Ira glanced at his wife, and then said, "You know, Noah, most people think we are a religion of cold, harsh laws, while Christianity is about love and brotherhood. Laws are the heart of our religion, but a large part of those laws are about love, and brotherhood, and the relationship between a man and his neighbors. There is a story told about Rabbi Hillel who lived around the time of Jesus. A pagan came to him saying that he would convert to Judaism if Hillel could teach him the first five books of your Bible which to us is called the Torah, in the time he could stand on one foot. Hillel replied, 'What is hateful to yourself, do not do to your fellow man. That is the whole Torah, all the rest is just commentary.' You see the golden rule didn't start with Christianity; it was a fundamental part of Judaism long before Hillel or Jesus," Ira concluded, looking at Noah. "I'm sorry, I didn't mean to get carried away," Ira said.

"No, no, I'm glad you did. I mean, I enjoyed it. I learned a lot." Noah said.

"I'll do the dishes. You two can go sit on the porch." Ruth said.

Noah took Ann's hand and led her to the settee swing on the porch. After they sat down, he held her in his arms and kissed her. "I like your family. Your uncle reminds me of Granddad. I bet they could talk each other to death," he said with a grin.

Ann laughed, "It's funny; when I was a little girl they came to visit us in Paris. When I first met uncle, I was scared to death. Rachael was still a toddler. She was so scared she ran and hid in the closet. We had to look all over the house for her. He had a way of appearing so gruff and," she said with a laugh, "my sister and I thought most Americans were Indians. Now I know that it is just his demeanor. He is really a kind, loving and gentle soul. My mother and aunt, being sisters, are very much alike, but my father and uncle are quite different. My father worked hard but he liked to play as well. He loved to take us on trips and to the theater and restaurants. Uncle is much more conservative, but I love them both."

Noah shook his head in acknowledgement. "I like all of them very much." He said.

"But you've never met my parents." Ann said.

"No, and I'm sorry that I won't have a chance to get to know your father, but I know them through you, and love them for giving you to me."

They sat quietly for a while, holding hands and listening to the night sounds of the frogs and cicadas, taking in the wonder and beauty of the world that was theirs.

Ira came out carrying a bottle of wine and three glasses. He poured the wine and gave them each one.

"L'chaim!" Ira said, lifting his glass.

"It means, 'To life,'" Ann told Noah.

"To life, 'L'chaim!'" Noah said, raising his glass.

CHAPTER 15

"Wake up, sleepy head, your breakfast is ready," Mary called to Noah.

Noah rolled over, stretching as he looked at the clock. It was after nine and he couldn't believe he had slept that late.

Jumping out of bed, he yelled, "Okay, I'll be right there." Walking over to the open window, he looked out on what promised to be another spectacular mountain day, with the warm, clean air sliding through the sunny skies, infusing itself with the scent of meadow flowers. He couldn't help feeling that this was a perfect day to start the next chapter of his life, with Ann.

He hurriedly dressed and went into the kitchen, where Mary and Thelma were hard at work preparing food for the party after the wedding.

"It sure smells good in here!" Noah exclaimed.

"Hope it'll taste that way too," Thelma responded.

"Sit down and eat. You're going to need your strength today," Mary said with a laugh.

"Not that again," Noah thought.

The day seemed interminably long for Noah since he was not allowed to see Ann before the wedding because the thought was it could bring them bad luck. Originally, the plan was to have a church wedding with a Minister and a Rabbi. Now, because of the short time, just the Justice of the Peace would perform the ceremony. Everyone agreed they would do it again with both ceremonies when Ann returned.

Finally, the time was drawing near and Noah finished changing into his suit. He, along with George and Sam, walked over to the church where the ceremony would be held. He hoped his nervousness was not too noticeable. He felt his neck to reassure himself that the claw necklace was there under his shirt. Noah stood beside the Justice of the Peace, Frank Haywood, who was conducting the marriage. Sam stood on the other side and seated in front of them were George, Mary and a number of the town folk.

Lucy Krebs, the church music director, sat at the piano that she had played for many a wedding in the little church and began to play "Here comes the Bride."

Noah looked up and saw Ann, escorted by Ira, and followed by Thelma. Her quiet beauty mesmerized him. Her long black hair, large dark eyes and scattering of freckles across the bridge of her nose, were contrasted by the pure white of her wedding gown. Around her neck was the medallion Noah had given her. Both she and Thelma wore a ring of wild flowers in their hair and carried bouquets from the same flowers that Mary had gathered from her garden. It had been decided that Mary's wedding gown would serve as something old and borrowed, and she wore a new pair of shoes. A blue ribbon was tied on the bouquet Ann carried.

Following Jewish tradition, both Ruth and Ira led Ann down the aisle, to a prayer shawl that Ira had furnished. It became a canopy or "chuppa" that was supported on poles held by four girls. When asked, Ira gave her away then he and Ruth returned to their seats. Thelma smiled at Sam, who smiled back and winked.

The ceremony was over much too quickly and everyone retired to George and Mary's for refreshments. While Ann and Noah changed clothes, Mary and Thelma took charge of setting out the food and drink for the party. After Ann emerged from the bedroom, she tossed her bouquet over her shoulder to the single women assembled. Much to the chagrin of the rest of the group, Lucy Krebs made a perfect leap and caught the bouquet in mid-air.

After everyone had eaten and visited for awhile, Ira got up and proposed a toast. Raising his glass of wine, he said, "The Talmud teaches that forty days before a male child is conceived, a voice from Heaven announces whose daughter he is going to marry, literally a match made in Heaven. In Yiddish this perfect match is called 'Bashert', a word that means fate or destiny. So, I drink to this union, these two soul mates, this 'Bashert'. Mazel Tov!"

Not to be outdone, George got up and lifted his glass. "May you have enough happiness to keep you sweet, enough trials to keep you strong, enough sorrow to keep you human, enough hope to keep you happy, enough failure to keep you humble, enough success to keep you eager, enough friends to give you comfort, enough faith and courage in yourself, your business, and your country to banish depression, enough wealth to meet your needs, and enough determination to make each day a better day than yesterday." As he drank, he looked at Ira. "Mazel Tov!" he shouted, smiling.

Sam stood up and walked over to Noah, announcing to everyone, "Thelma and me had planned on Noah and Ann getting married with us, but even though that didn't happen, I want to share something with them." Sam put his arm around Noah's shoulder, and Thelma held Ann's hand as they led them down the street, with everyone following, to the park. There was a hole dug in the ground, and lying beside it was a tree.

"We have a tradition where I come from of planting a 'wedding' tree," Sam explained, as he led Noah and Ann over to where the tree lay. Together, Noah and Ann placed the tree into the hole and then filled the hole with dirt. "May its roots, like this marriage, go deep into the fertile ground to hold it in place against the storms of life. May it grow many strong limbs like the children that will come, and may its fruit be plentiful." Everyone was impressed with Sam's eloquence, but later he confessed to Thelma that he had memorized it.

Everyone applauded and then walked back up the street to the reception: Sam holding Thelma's hand, and Noah, with his arm around Ann. As George took pictures with his Kodak Brownie camera he said, "We can show these to your parents, and send some to Ann's family." Everyone ate and drank until it was finally time for Noah and Ann to leave. They planned to drive to the city, spend the night and the next morning Noah would take Ann to the train before he came back.

George gave Noah the keys to his car and checked to make sure Ann's bags were already loaded. They said their goodbyes and jumped into the car; Noah turned to Ann and said. "Hello, Mrs. Johnson."

"Hello, Mr. Johnson," she replied, smiling sweetly.

They kissed, and everyone hollered, prompting Noah to drive off quickly, with the obligatory string of tin cans clanging and a "Just Married" sign on the back of the car. Noah and Ann laughed, as they drove away, but as soon as they were out of town they stopped to remove the cans but left the sign. The rest of the drive, Ann sat next to Noah, her head on his chest and his arm around her. They made small talk, reliving the events of the past couple of days. Neither wanted to think about tomorrow nor what the future might bring.

Neither Noah nor Ann hurried to get up the next morning, knowing that they would soon be parted. Noah was the first to awaken, and he lay there studying Ann, thinking how beautiful she was with the sunlight playing across her face. He thanked God for bringing her into his life.

"Come on sleepy head, we have to get up," he said, as he gently tousled his wife's hair.

"I don't want to. I want to stay here with you," she said with a yawn. "We could make love day and night," Ann said, as she pushed the sheet down. Clad only in a pair of silk panties, her long legs, firm midriff, and pert breasts were exposed.

"Whoa tiger, I'll have to eat something to keep up my strength! In fact, I'm hungry right now," he said, getting up and walking to the table where flowers, an unopened bottle of champagne, and chocolates were placed. His Grandparents had arranged for them, along with the room, as a wedding present. He wolfed down several of the chocolates before returning to the bed.

"I'll bet I can make you forget about your hunger," she murmured, reaching over and stroking him.

"What hunger?" he said, laughing, as he gathered her into his arms.

They finally had to face reality and get up. Noah picked up the bottle of champagne, "We'll keep this and open it when you return." He said.

They dressed and Noah loaded the car. After removing what remained of the sign, they drove to the station. On the way, Ann sat quietly beside him with tears in her eyes.

"It's going to be okay," Noah said, trying to be reassuring. "You'll only be gone a short time and then we can be together, forever," he said.

"And a day?" Ann said, trying to smile bravely through her tears.

"And a day," Noah said, drawing her to him. "You'll let me know when you get there?"

"I promise. I love you so, Darling." She said.

They hugged and kissed until she was forced to board. Noah watched as she found a seat next to the window. They pressed their hands together through the glass until the train started to move. Noah watched as the train pulled away and waited until it went out of sight, and then began the drive back to Fairview. It felt to him that it was a lot longer going back than it had been coming.

When Noah arrived, an enormous tiredness came over him. It seemed that the weight of the world rested on him. He went to his room and lay down on the bed, where he remained the rest of the day. The next morning, he moped around all day, unable to be enthusiastic about anything

"I'm worried about Noah," Mary said to George later that evening.

"Me too. He is obviously depressed," George said. "I think I'll see if I can talk him into going fishing with me in the morning. "

"That's a great idea, sweetheart," Mary said, squeezing his arm.

Noah finally acquiesced after much cajoling from George. They decided to get an early start, before it got too hot. In the heat of the day, the insects dispersed and the trout stopped feeding. Noah was fascinated by the morning mist that hung in sheets over the meadow, taking on the appearance of billowing whitecaps on an inland sea. The rising sun would soon burn off the moisture, banishing it back into the sky. The sun was reflecting on the undersides of wispy clouds, infusing them with pale pinks, creams, and blues. For a few moments, he felt at peace. George and Noah put on their waders and stepped into the stream, standing slightly apart and at angles to each other. They talked about the day and of recent events. George passed on the news that while Noah was gone, President Roosevelt had announced that Thanksgiving was being changed from November 30 to the 23, to help retailers by having extra time before Christmas.

"Makes you wonder if people have forgotten why we celebrate Christmas," George said.

As they continued to fish, Noah noticed his grandfather studying him.

"You know Noah; life is a lot like fishing. We keep showing up and casting our line into the stream, not knowing if we'll catch anything or not. A lot of times we don't, but if we keep doing it, every once in a while, we become a winner and make a spectacular catch. It's those times that we will fall back on and remember through all those other bad, disappointing times." George said.

Noah nodded he understood what was being said.

"You're right, Grandfather. I guess I'm just down on everything. I'm having what I have heard you refer to as a 'pity party'. I should be on cloud nine. I'm here in this spectacular setting and I'm married to the most wonderful, beautiful, woman in the whole world. It's not like she's gone forever. In a few months she'll be back and we'll have the rest of our lives together," Noah said hopefully.

As they spent the rest of the morning fishing, Noah felt his spirits begin to rise. The fishing had been mediocre. Having caught only three fish, one Rainbow and two Brookies, they decided to call it a day.

"Thanks," Noah said as they walked home.

"What for?" George asked.

"For making me realize just how lucky I am and how much I have to live for and to look forward to." Noah replied.

CHAPTER 16

Noah became more restless as the days went by. Even fishing with his grandfather no longer held his interest. Except for the one telegram from Ann that he received after her arrival, he had heard nothing.

George was worried about Noah. He came to the conclusion that Noah needed a way to keep his mind off of Ann, so he decided to ask him to help in the clinic. At first Noah protested, but George pleaded, saying he was not feeling well and could really use the help.

"I don't know how much help I would be. I won't know what to do," Noah responded.

"Just assist me, you know, get me what I need and help me with the routine things," George explained, hoping to reassure Noah.

Noah finally agreed and they went into the clinic, which was attached to the side of the house by a breezeway. When they opened the door, the office waiting room was full.

"Typical Monday," George said. "Let's get busy."

They worked steadily all morning. Noah, with George's help, cleaned, disinfected, and bandaged, a leg and arm injury on Johnny Peterson, the result of a fall from his bike. He watched as George stitched a scalp wound and administered a tetanus shot to a fisherman who's wound was sustained from an errant lure. They examined a child with a cold, and gave a sulfa drug to Joseph Hartley, who was suffering from a urinary infection. They treated various other ailments and assorted aches and pains and, in an emergency, Noah assisted George in setting a broken arm.

The morning went by fast. They took a break for a quick lunch, and then went back to work. When they finally saw the last patient, Noah was exhausted, but felt good about being able to help the people he loved. A lot of the patients could not pay for their treatment and were allowed to provide goods and services instead. Noah did not tell George but he now knew, beyond a doubt, that this was what he wanted to do with his life.

"How do you feel?" George asked, putting his arm around Noah.

"Tired, but I enjoyed it. Thanks," Noah said.

George did not mention it, but he could tell Noah had forgotten his own problems. The clinic was open three days a week, except for emergencies and Noah found himself actually looking forward to those days. When he was not working in the clinic, he would go fishing, spend time in Ira's drugstore, or visit Sam, who was becoming increasingly anxious about his upcoming wedding to Thelma. At the end of the first week, Noah told his grandfather he had decided he wanted to become a doctor.

"I told Ann before she left that I was thinking about it. She thought it was a great idea. If it's okay with you, we would like to come back here to live. I could help you in your practice." Noah said.

His grandfather was elated. "I can think of nothing I would want more. It's what I have been praying for. Looks like I made the right choice when I gave you that medical dictionary for your birthday." He insisted that Noah should make application right away, and that he would write a letter to the dean of the medical school located where Noah lived.

Noah went to the drugstore to see if Ira had heard from Ann. "I haven't heard anything; I'm really worried. They said on the radio last night that Germany and Russia had signed a non-aggression pact. I'm afraid that gives Hitler a green light to do what he wants," Ira said.

"You think Ann's in danger?" Noah asked, apprehensively.

"I don't know, probably not. I think Hitler's looking at the Baltic areas, not France. Aren't your parents coming soon?" Ira said, changing the subject.

"Yes sir, they're coming for Thelma and Sam's wedding next week." Noah responded.

Several days later, Noah finally received a letter from Ann.

My Darling Noah,
I am sorry I have not written earlier. I have had to take care of my father's affairs and help my mother and sister. There's so much to do. Everything is hectic around here. The government called up the military reserves and put wartime measures in effect. Most of the children have been evacuated out of Paris to the countryside.
My darling, I don't want you to think I am in a panic, but I have to admit, I am somewhat worried about the situation and am staying alert, although I do not see any immediate

danger. I am trying to hurry (through everything so I can come back home (my new one) to you.

I keep thinking sweet thoughts of you and our 'special place' at Fairview. Maybe we can go on a picnic and open that bottle of champagne. You are still my King and I am now your Queen for real. I have learned one thing; that the few weeks we had together are better than a lifetime without you.

Noah, give my love to your family, especially your grandparents. Tell Thelma and Sam I am sorry I will miss their wedding, but look forward to seeing them before long. Please let my Uncle and Aunt know you heard from me and that all the family is okay.

Darling, I will write again soon, but in the meantime, please know that I love you more than life itself. I will always love you, forever and a day.

Your loving wife,

Ann

After Noah shared the news from Ann's letter, George said, "I don't like it. I hope Ann comes home soon. I'm afraid that non-aggression pact means there is nothing to stop Hitler now."

This was disheartening to Noah, especially since he had heard both Mr. Zimmerman and his grandfather express the same fears. He could not get it out of his mind. Even the approaching wedding of Sam and Thelma could not cheer him up. He wrote Ann as soon as he could, begging her to come home.

My dearest Ann,

I cannot tell you in words how much I miss you. It seems so unfair that just as we found each other, we have to be separated. It is too cruel. I know you have a responsibility and I am being selfish, but I can't help it. I still wish that I had gone with you. I hope we have done the right thing. I thought about going back to our "special place", but I think it would be too depressing without you so I will wait for your return.

Everyone here sends their love. Sam and Thelma are making the final preparations for their wedding. Sam is as nervous as a long-tailed cat in a room full of rocking chairs.

Granddad and I have been talking to him, trying to calm him down. He is worried that he isn't good enough for Thelma, but I have told him that I have learned, thanks to you, that if you love someone as much as we love each other, then everything else will take care of itself.

I have been helping Granddad in the clinic, and it has reinforced my desire to go to medical school and then for us to come back here to live. I'll be leaving right after the wedding to go back home and start medical school. Dad says we can fix up the room over the garage and live there. Please hurry home as soon as you can, so we can open that bottle of champagne.

You are right, my love, a few days spent with you is better than a lifetime without you.

All my love, forever, and a day,

Noah

The wedding plans were all in place. Noah's parents arrived and Noah would be leaving with them the next day. As usual, Louise took charge. She, along with Mary and Thelma, sat down to put the finishing touches on the plans. They would be married at the Methodist church and the whole town was invited. Neither Sam nor Thelma had any family that would be attending.

"Thelma, what are you planning on wearing for the wedding?" Mary asked.

"I thought I would wear one of my church dresses." Thelma replied.

"Nonsense, I want you to wear the gown that I gave Ann to wear," Mary said. Louise started to protest but Mary quickly continued, "I asked Noah and he thought Ann would be honored for you to use it."

"Oh, Miss Mary, I don't know. Are you sure? Besides, I'm not sure it will fit." Thelma said.

"Of course, my dear, it would make us all happy. God knows we all could use some cheering up. Don't worry about it fitting. We'll just let out the darts and if we have to, I can add a little on the sides." Mary said.

Louise looked dejected. "Thank you, I sure appreciate it. I can't tell you how much it means to me. I love you and Ann." Thelma said, then added as an afterthought, "You too, Miss Louise." Louise nodded, avoiding eye contact.

Sam, Noah and George were talking in the other room.

"I'm really nervous," Sam said. "When my ancestors got married they just jumped over a broom stick. Sure would be a lot easier!" George and Noah laughed.

"Women want us to suffer so we'll know who really is in charge," George said with a chuckle.

"I just hope I'm good enough for her," Sam mused.

"You're wondering about it tells me you will do just fine," George said, putting his arm around Sam's shoulder.

Sam turned to Noah, "Have you heard anything more from Ann?"

"No, not a word," Noah said, shaking his head glumly.

"I wish she was here," Sam said.

"Me too," Noah answered, "Me too."

Everyone was up bright and early for the wedding. Noah was best man and Michael was a groomsman, protesting loudly about having to wear a suit. They asked Louise to be the maid of honor, but she declined saying she was not feeling well. Mary agreed to fill in. George was asked to give the bride away and he happily agreed. "Of course, my dear," he told her. "Nothing would give me greater pleasure."

The wedding went off without a hitch, almost. Sam was so nervous that he dropped the ring, and Michael had to scurry around to retrieve it; an event for which Sam had to endure a lot of good-natured ribbing. Everyone agreed it was a wonderful wedding. Noah, however, felt sad and, surprisingly had an ominous feeling as he watched. Afterwards, there was a big party at the pavilion with food and drinks, along with dancing to music provided by several local musicians. As soon as the ceremony was over, Sam and Thelma planted a wedding tree of their own next to the one Noah and Ann had planted.

Sam spoke to the gathered crowd.

"Thelma and me are planting this tree as we begin our life together. We are planting it next to the one Noah and Ann planted. Two trees representing two families who will grow and blossom together. May we always have sunny days and gentle rain."

Noah went up to him afterwards and thanked him. "It's going to be all right," Sam said, putting his arm around Noah.

As the afternoon progressed, George kept an eye on Noah and noticed he was becoming increasingly anxious. He saw Noah standing on the steps, looking at the sky, and walked over and joined him.

"You okay?" George asked.

"I was just looking at the clouds." Noah turned and faced George. "Ann once asked me if I thought that someone on the other side of the world could see the same clouds."

George took a deep breath and said, "I don't know about clouds, but I do know that the power of love reaches everywhere. You can't stop it from finding you, no matter where you are." George put his arm around Noah. "She's going to be all right. Ann's a smart girl and can take care of herself."

Noah smiled, trying desperately to hide the anxiety on his face.

CHAPTER 17

The next morning Noah and his family left for home. Noah had mixed feelings as they left. On the one hand, he loved it here, along with the good memories of his friends and especially Ann. On the other hand, his recent separation from Ann was still too painful, leaving a hole in his heart and the letters he had received from her only added to his sense of foreboding and loss. George and Mary prepared a big breakfast and fixed a lunch for Noah and the others as they packed the car for the trip home. Sam and Thelma came by to say good-bye.

"I'm sure goin' to miss you," Sam said to Noah. "I hope you come back real soon," then added, "with Ann."

"I hope so too," Noah answered, hugging him and then embracing Thelma.

"You take care of him," Noah told Thelma, with a wink.

"It's going to be a full-time job," she said with a smile. Thelma's look grew serious. "We'll keep you and Ann in our prayers."

"Thanks," Noah responded, and then thought, "I hope God is listening."

Noah kissed his grandmother, then turned to his grandfather and hugged him, not wanting to let go. "I'm going to miss you and this place."

"You'll be back," George said prophetically, "It's in your heart and blood. There is an old saying 'Don't cry because it's over – smile because it happened.'"

Noah laughed, "You always know the right words, Granddad. I probably should write them down." Noah said, hugging his Grandfather.

"Just listen with your heart and you'll be okay," George advised.

"We need to go," Louise said impatiently. "Come on Arthur," she shouted as she pulled Michael into the car and got in herself.

Arthur followed and then turned and gave the keys to Noah. "You drive," he said, and added as he elbowed Noah, "but watch out for the chickens." He laughed.

"Thanks Dad," Noah said with a laugh, grateful to have something to keep his mind occupied. Noah slid into the driver's seat. "Boy this is a really nice car," he said, patting the dash of the new Buick. As they drove off, Noah looked back and saw the four people he loved most, besides Ann, David and his family standing together waving as the car moved away down the road.

"I will be back," he thought.

His mother sat in the front seat with him, while his father sat in back with Michael. For a while they drove in silence, until his mother began to talk.

"Well, I'll certainly be glad to get back home. Noah, I'm so glad you decided to apply to medical school."

"I don't know if I'll go," Noah said.

"What do you mean? I want you to go. I thought you had decided that's what you wanted. What else would you do?" she asked.

"I'm not sure, I just don't know if I'm ready to go back to school. Besides, I need to figure out what I am going to do about Ann," He said.

"Don't be silly. Ann's a big girl and perfectly capable of taking care of herself. You need to get on with your life. Ann chose to go back to France, to her own kind, and you have to go on without her," She said, very bluntly.

Noah had had enough.

"Mother, shut up," he said.

"Noah!" She said, shocked. She turned to the back seat. "Arthur, are you going to let him talk to me like that?"

Arthur looked at her with disgust. "Louise, I love you, but in this case you need to be quiet." He then said to Noah, "We will figure something out."

Noah smiled, feeling proud of his father. Louise sat with her hand over her mouth stunned for a moment, then turned and looked out the window. The rest of the trip was spent in relative silence.

When they pulled up to their house, Noah's best friend, David Lewis was waiting on the front steps.

"Hey man, glad you're back," he said, jumping up and giving Noah a hug.

"Good to see you," Noah answered. But in truth, except for seeing David, he was not excited to be there, especially without Ann.

"I'll give you a hand," David said, and began helping to unload the car.

"Thank you for your help," Louise told David after everything was inside.

"Glad I could help," David answered.

Arthur looked at them. "We can put everything up. Why don't you two go visit."

"Thanks. We will," Noah said, glad for the chance to get away and to reconnect with David. They went outside and as they sat down on the front porch, David was the first to speak.

"Boy, you certainly had a busy summer. I'm sorry I couldn't come to the wedding. I couldn't get that much time off since I just started my job."

"That's ok, it was hurried up," Noah replied. "No, not that," he said with a laugh, after David gave him a quizzical look. He went on to explain about Ann having to go back to Paris.

"Man, that's a real drag. Do you have her picture?" David asked.

Noah reached into his hip pocket and took out his billfold. He looked fondly at the picture of Ann that George had taken at the wedding and handed it to David.

"Man," exclaimed David, "she's the cat's meow. Tell me about her. How did you meet? Is she blind? She must be to marry an ugly S.O.B. like you!"

Noah laughed, and then spent the next half hour relating all he could. When he recounted the story of the cougar, David whistled. Noah showed him the claw necklace and David held it admiringly, before handing it back. When he finished, David studied him, then said with sincerity, "You must love her a lot. I'm sorry we didn't get to meet," then added, "but I know we will soon." Noah nodded, wanting to change what was becoming too painful a subject.

"What about you?" Noah asked. "Are you seeing anyone? Tell me about your new job."

David spent the next few minutes bringing Noah up to date. Noah studied his friend as he talked. They were nothing alike. David was a little shorter than he, but had a muscular body and possessed rugged good looks. Unlike Noah, he had no trouble finding girls to date. In fact, they usually found him. David had never been studious, while Noah had graduated with honors a year early. Noah had spent many nights helping David with his homework and even though Noah was one year younger, they had finished together. It seemed incongruous to their peers that the two of them were such good friends. Noah had always felt that it was a case of their personalities feeding off each other and making them stronger. They talked a little longer and then decided to go get a malt.

"Come on", Noah said. "We'll take my car."

"Your car?" David asked incredulously.

"Yeah, my parents gave Ann and me their old car as a wedding present."

"Neat." David said. They drove to the drugstore and went to the soda fountain and sat down in a booth.

A pretty blond girl in a pink dress came over to take their order.

"Hi David; what can I get you and your friend?" She asked.

"Hi Jo Lynn; this is, Noah Johnson. Could you please bring us two chocolate malts?"

She nodded to Noah as she left and returned a few minutes later with the malts. "I enjoyed the other night," she said coyly to David, popping her chewing gum and giving him a wink. "Call me. I'd love to do it again. Nice to meet you, Noah," she said as she left.

"Seems like a nice girl," Noah said.

"Oh, she's okay I guess, just pray she never gets caught in a rainstorm. She'd drown before she ever figured out how to stay dry," David said, shaking his head. Changing the subject, he asked. "So, tell me, what are you planning on doing now that you've graduated and gotten yourself married?"

"I want to go to medical school and then move back to Fairview and take over for my grandfather in his clinic," Noah answered, having made up his mind on the drive back home. "It's what I want, and it's what Ann wants too."

"You could make a lot more money practicing somewhere else," David said.

"Yeah, you're right, but I wouldn't be as happy and neither would Ann. We both love Fairview and feel a certain connection there. It's as if we were meant to meet, fall in love, marry and live the rest of our lives right there. I realized that this summer, being there with Ann and my grandparents."

"I can't believe you got married. What's it like?" David asked.

"It's great, even though we didn't have much time together. We both realize that it's right for us and that soon we'll have the rest of our lives to make up for lost time. I guess it gives us something to live for and look forward to. Maybe that's why it feels so good." Noah said. "Enough about me, us, tell me about you. What about this job?"

David explained that, "it was just a job," and he was not excited about it and was still looking around.

When Noah got back home, he went to his room. It was just as he had left it a few months earlier, yet oddly it now seemed an alien place. He didn't feel this was where he belonged. In fact, he felt a strange detachment and sense of unreality. He spent some time putting away his stuff and resigned himself to settle in and move forward with his plan to enroll in medical school. It was no longer for himself; he now felt he owed it to Ann and to their future.

That night, his father noticed Noah as he sat on the porch staring up at the sky.

"What do you see?" His father asked, placing his hand on Noah's shoulder to get his attention.

"Oh nothing, I was just looking at the stars, wondering who else sees them." He did not mention Ann, even though she was in his thoughts.

Noah applied for medical school and because of his grades and his grandfather's glowing recommendation was accepted and enrolled. Life began settling into a routine as he buried himself in his studies and found solace in the distraction they offered. The war news seemed to settle down a bit and Noah began to think that maybe there would be peace after all, but he still could not shake his feeling of apprehension and loss. It was like being in an unfamiliar land. He was physically there, but his heart and mind were someplace else. He was becoming an emotional disaster. He found some solace in writing Ann about the wedding, his coming home, and his enrollment in medical school. Every day he waited for the mail; hoping, praying, for some word from Ann.

September arrived with both renewed hope and hopelessness. Germany invaded Poland and three days later, France and England declared war against Germany. Noah was thrilled when a letter from Ann arrived, along with a new photograph of her with the Eiffel Tower in the background. It arrived weeks after it was written, which concerned Noah.

August, 1939
My Darling,
    I miss you so very, very much. Please do not worry about me, I am fine. Mother is doing much better. Rachel is back in school. I have been caring for mother, helping her

get her life back in order. I am so happy for Thelma and Sam. I hope they find the same happiness in each other as you and I have found. I plan to come back home (it is you know) soon, once everything is settled.

I trust everyone, especially you, my darling, is doing well. I am so proud of you for enrolling in medical school. Noah, you must follow your (our) dream. It's what you are and now, I am a part of it. How I long to be back in Fairview, lying in the grass at our special place, holding each other. Oh well, that thought is the one thing that makes this bearable for now. I hope someday we can come here and I can show you "The City of Light"- my beautiful Paris. Don't worry, I wouldn't trade Fairview for it, but it is still magical. My darling, this will all be over soon and we will have the rest of our lives to make up for all the lost time. In the meantime, just remember I will love you forever, and a day.

Your loving wife (how wonderful to be able to write that),
Ann

Rather than cheer him up, Ann's letter made him more depressed. For once he was glad to be enrolled in school. It was his only outlet and he devoted all of his time to it. Still, he could not help worrying about her. He kept blaming himself for not going with her to Paris, although in more rational moments he realized staying here made more sense at the time. He wrote every week but never received a reply. Thanksgiving arrived, but it only made Noah more anxious. He hated the respite, not feeling he had anything to be thankful for. He began to feel even more despondent as Christmas approached. Finally, a week before Christmas, he received another letter from Ann.

December, 1939
Dearest Noah,

I have been receiving all your letters and have wanted to write back to you, but it is hard since all the mail is prioritized and quite expensive. I have taken a Job in a bookstore and am saving money for the trip back to you. miss you so much, my darling. I am afraid Rachael and mother have grown tired of listening to me telling them how wonderful you are. I am glad your studies are going well. You must keep at it. It will mean so much to us and our future when we go back to Fairview. How I long for that day.

Everything is okay so far here. I know you are aware that we are at war with Germany. Sometimes it seems as if I am living out a self-fulfilling prophecy.

Life is going on, even though there are shortages of some things. The lack of gasoline has forced many, including myself, to ride bicycles.

My legs are getting very strong, so I guess some good has come of that. We are all making do, so please do not worry; I hope to be back home with you before long. Keep that bottle of champagne cold.

Merry Christmas, my love, and wish everyone the same. I love you more than life itself, forever, and a day.
Your loving wife,
Ann

Christmas came and with it all the reminders of home and family. This should have been a joyous occasion; his first Christmas as a married man. Instead, he felt an overwhelming sense of loss. Christmas Eve, Noah and his family went to church. After the service, Noah excused himself by saying he just wanted to walk a little. He went to the Jewish synagogue, where he stood outside and offered up a prayer, asking God, the God of all people, to watch over and protect Ann.

The next morning the family gathered in the living room to open their presents. Noah received a new fountain pen, a sweater, an anatomy book and, a painting of him and Ann that his grandparents had made from a picture. The painting touched his heart. Louise insisted they pick up all the wrappings and clean up before they ate breakfast. Louise had hired a new housekeeper named Ruth, who had spent the previous day cooking, so Louise would only have to heat everything up and not "tire herself out in a hot kitchen."

They sat down to breakfast and before long, much to Louise's chagrin, the talk turned to the world situation.

"I don't think the French and British can stop Hitler," Arthur said, and then looked at Noah. "Of course, I could be way off base."

"I hope we get into the fight. Man, I'd like to go over there and kick Hitler in the as--uh, seat of the pants," said Michael.

"Michael!" his mother admonished. "I personally hope no American boy has to fight. It's not our war."

"Whose is it? Is it Ann's?" Noah asked.

"Oh Noah, you know I don't blame Ann, but the Jews have created a big problem, and Ann certainly was aware of what she was getting into. Besides, I think the French and English will win. After all they are much more civilized." Louise retorted.

Noah looked at her for a moment, shaking his head. "You're unbelievable. If we do end up in a war, I hope people like you have nothing to do with it. If we did, we would lose, and everyone else will be to blame." He put his napkin on the table and got up. "Excuse me, I need some fresh air." Noah said, turning from the table abruptly.

"Well, what's the matter with him?" she asked, mystified. Arthur just shook his head.

CHAPTER 18

The days rolled by in a slow, methodical, progression. Noah immersed himself in school and yet, like a drowning man, thoughts and worries about Ann, kept bobbing to the surface. Nineteen forty did nothing to dispel those fears. In the spring, Germany continued its blitzkrieg, first rolling into Denmark and Norway, then the Netherlands, Belgium and Luxembourg. May brought news of the defeat and evacuation of the British Expeditionary Force along with remnants of the French First Army at Dunkirk. There was a lot of jubilation over their rescue, but Winston Churchill doused that enthusiasm by saying, "Wars are not won by evacuations." The worst news came a few weeks later, in mid-June, with the fall of Paris, and then the surrender of France. Noah was beside himself with worry. Finally, after another month went by, he received a letter from Ann.

> My Darling Noah,
>   I am writing to you with a heavy heart. My beloved Paris is no more the "City of Light." Darkness fell over it today as German troops strutted down the Champs d'Elysee.
>   The Germans removed our flags and replaced them with that horrid swastika. They placed signs on the Eiffel Tower and the Chamber of Deputies that read in German "Germany conquers on all fronts." I am trying to be brave for us but I have to admit it is hard to do. So far, except for some shortages, it has been okay. I suppose it is the uncertainty that is the worst. I would like to leave, but the only way out is to the South and that is not safe. Human vultures are demanding fortunes in gold to transport people in their cars and German Stukas frequently sweep down from the sky to prey on easy targets.
>   My darling, I am not sure if, or when, I will be able to contact you again. I hope you receive this letter. I had to bribe someone to take it South with them. Please do not

worry about me. Darling, for both our sakes, you must go on
with your studies and your life.

That thought is the one thing that makes all this bearable.
I will try to be strong, knowing that this will be over
someday and we can at last open that bottle of champagne.
Give my love to your family, Sam and Thelma, and
especially your grandparents.

Remember my love; I love you with all my heart, forever,
and a day.

Your loving wife,

Ann

The next summer came and went with no more news from Ann.
The Battle of Britain roared on, as did Noah's own battle with his
worry about Ann. Towards the end of the year, the British drove the
Italian Army out of Egypt. In September, Roosevelt signed into law
the Selective Training and Service Act, requiring all men between
twenty-one and thirty-five to register for military service. This
became known as "The Draft," and both Noah and David signed up.
If you were selected it was supposed to be for one year and service
only in the Western hemisphere. Later Noah would remember the
irony of a popular song "Don't Worry Dear, I'll Be Back in a Year."

Nineteen forty-one arrived, and still the war dragged on.
Roosevelt was able to get a lend-lease bill passed, allowing aid to
Britain and other Allied nations. The German battleship Bismarck
was sunk, and in June Hitler surprised everyone by invading the
Soviet Union.

December finally came, and Noah was not looking forward to
another holiday without Ann. He was in the last week of school
before the Christmas break. It was a Sunday morning and, as was
his habit, he was sleeping late.
Suddenly there was a knock on the door.

"Yeah," Noah said in a voice still groggy with sleep.

"Hey man, open up. Did you hear the news?" Michael said.

"No, go away." Noah said.

"You'll want to hear this. The Japanese just attacked Pearl
Harbor. It's all over the radio. Looks like they sunk a number of
our ships. Dad said all hell is going to break loose." Michael said
excitably.

Noah jumped up, threw on some clothes, and ran into the living
room where his father and mother were huddled around the radio.

He started to say something but his father made a gesture for quiet. His mother was crying.

"The Japanese have bombed Pearl Harbor Hawaii in Hawaii. Looks like we are in a war." Arthur said astonished by the news.

Noah sat there listening, knowing intuitively that his life was about to change drastically. It wasn't until later that they realized no one had mentioned breakfast and it had passed, forgotten.

The next day, Roosevelt delivered his speech and declared December 7th would be, "A day that would live in infamy." Congress declared war on Japan, Germany, and Italy.

That afternoon David came by. "Hey man, can you believe those Japs would do something that stupid? Man, we're going to kick their little yellow asses," David vented.

"I don't know," Noah said. "I don't think it's going to be that easy. Our fleet is sunk, and we also have the Germans and Italians to deal with."

"Well, I want to get in there and pay them back." David looked at Noah. "Can you keep a secret?"

"I guess so, sure," Noah replied.

"I'm going to enlist." David paused a moment, then continued, "Why don't you join up with me?"

"I want to, Noah paused a moment and said "I've been thinking about it, but I have to be in Europe where I can look for Ann. Why don't you come and enlist with me?" Noah said.

"Japs, Germans, Italians. I don't guess it makes a lot of difference. What the shit, they're all the enemy. Let's do it! Besides, I want to meet Ann and find out just what she sees in a crazy son-of-a-bitch like you." David said, and slapped Noah on the back.

The Secretary of the Army made a special plea to the deans of various medical schools to institute an accelerated curriculum and allow students to graduate early. Because they had not received their MD, these students could not be doctors, but corpsmen. Noah asked and was made a Medical Corpsman. David did the same so he could serve in the same outfit as Noah and to their great relief, was accepted as an aid and stretcher-bearer. When Noah told his parents about his enlistment, his mother cried and insisted he did not have to go. His father hugged him and told him how proud he was. He made Noah promise to be careful and not take unnecessary chances. Michael just said "Wow!" and asked if Noah would bring him a Lugar, which made his mother cry even more.

Later that day, as Louise and Arthur sat in their living room, Louise asked, "What would make Noah do such a stupid thing?" She sat, staring at the floor, wringing her hands.

"I guess it was a sense of duty and maybe his desire to try and locate Ann." Arthur said.

Louise shook her head in disbelief.

Arthur continued, "We raised a good son who has grown into a fine young man. I'm proud of him and you should be too. I remember when I was teaching him to ride a bicycle. I would run along, holding onto him to keep him from falling. Then one day I let go so he could do it on his own. At first he didn't realize I had let go but when he did you could see the joy and confidence in his face. That's what we have to do now; just let him go and take that ride."

Noah was allowed to finish his semester in medical school and David waited to enlist with Noah. Then he and David boarded a bus to go and begin basic training. Leaving home was bittersweet, but in a way he was glad for the diversion and the thought that it would bring him nearer to Ann elated him.

Noah and David were shipped to the newly activated Medical Replacement Training Center at Camp Robinson in Arkansas. Here they went through seventeen weeks of basic training. In addition to their medical training, they were instructed in subjects such as hand-to-hand combat, demolition, how to identify and avoid booby-trap and mines, village fighting, and knots and lashings

Commanders were urged to move trainees into the field and train them under simulated combat conditions. A few days after arrival the trainees were marched to a natural amphitheater in the woods. They watched the staging of a mock battle in which medics moved forward to treat simulated casualties. Sound effects were provided by dynamite blasts and amplified recordings of bombs, artillery, and small arms fire. While the cast played their part, a narrator indoctrinated the trainees in the combat mission of medical soldiers.

"Is it too late to join the Navy?" David asked.

In early 1942, after completing their training, they waited for their deployment orders to arrive. Noah, David, and the rest of their battalion, some 40,000 men, shipped out of Boston harbor, headed for England. Their convoy of forty-three ships was guarded by twelve destroyers, which would offer protection against German U-boat attacks. Noah noticed that the Battleship Texas, a relic from the First World War, was accompanying them, in case of a direct attack. Somehow, seeing that old ship made him think of Sam, who had fought in the First World War, and of his grandfather. There seemed a certain degree of comfort in having that experience from the past with them.

Just in case a "Wolf Pack" of German submarines succeeded in sinking their ship, Noah and all the other men were instructed to remain fully dressed at all times over two-piece woolen underwear and wear their life jackets twenty-four hours a day to improve their chances of survival if their ship went down in the icy Atlantic.

"I think I would rather take my chances in the Atlantic than to have to wear this hot, itchy, stinking underwear," David remarked, scratching himself vigorously.

Noah just laughed, knowing it was useless to try to talk logically to him. Noah would go top-side at night to cool off. The ship was running without lights which only served to highlight the brilliance of the stars in the night sky ablaze with the light of a thousand galaxies. The shimmering starlight took his thoughts back to Fairview and summer nights spent holding Ann.

Noah and David witnessed several ships sinking after being torpedoed. One was very close to their ship. It must have been carrying munitions, since it exploded on impact. They could hear the screams of the men who were on fire and watched horrified, as they jumped overboard.

"Those poor bastards," David said, shaking his head.

It was a sobering reminder that this was deadly serious. Noah prayed that he would live long enough to find Ann and hold her in his arms once again.

The battalion finally reached England after eight days and the loss of six ships. The men were taken off the ships, loaded on trucks, and transported to a rural area where they were billeted in an old abandoned warehouse. They set up a makeshift hospital and bivouac around it. A few days after their arrival, David became one of the first patients to be treated. He had borrowed a bicycle to "check out" the local girls. The bike he had ridden back home had the brakes in the pedals, but the English brakes were located on the bicycle handlebars. There was a turn at the bottom of a hill and when he tried to put back pressure on the pedals, they just rotated. He could not stop and collided head first into a fence, sustaining numerous cuts and contusions. Noah gave him a hard time about becoming the first casualty.

"Maybe you will be given a purple heart for risking life and limb above and beyond the call of duty in pursuit of the opposite sex!" Noah said, laughing as he treated David's wounds.

David responded, saying, "The next time I'll see if I can find a sailor who will give me an anchor to drag for a brake."

Noah, David and thousands of others trained and tried to fight off boredom. David passed his time by playing poker and losing all his pay. Everyone knew a massive invasion was coming, but its precise timing and location were kept in utmost secrecy. All leaves were cancelled and they were confined to the base. Noah looked forward to the letters he received from his mother, full of the news about life at home.

> Dear Noah,
>
> I hope you are doing well and taking good care of yourself. Everything is okay here. I am working with the USO, helping in their canteens and also aiding in selling war bonds. I am really excited since I learned The Andrew Sisters are going to be here for a bond rally. Your dad is serving on the local draft board and Michael is helping to organize scrap metal drives. The big news is that Thelma is pregnant. I don't know how they can afford to have a child, but I guess that is their problem. The baby is due in six months and Sam is driving her crazy with his doting on her.
>
> Your grandparents are well, although George is having trouble with his arthritis. He told me to tell you to hurry up and win the war so you can take over his practice. I hope you will consider locating in a city. It would be easier and you would make more money. He asked me to send you the enclosed envelope.
>
> Your dad and Michael send their love. Michael says to tell you not to forget his Lugar.
> Love,
> Mother

Inside the envelope was a small fly his grandfather had tied along with a note saying how he looked forward to Noah and Ann coming back so they could all go fishing and how the next time maybe he and Ann would take pity on Noah and let him catch the biggest fish.

With a chuckle Noah put the fly inside his helmet. The only thing missing was a letter from Ann.

CHAPTER 19

Finally, in June of 1944, they were ordered to break camp and move to the docks at South Hampton. They were read a message from General Eisenhower.

> Soldiers, sailors and airmen of the allied expeditionary force, you are about to embark upon the great crusade toward which we have striven these many months. The eyes of the world are upon you. Good luck and let us all beseech the blessings of Almighty God upon this great and noble undertaking.
> Gen. Dwight D. Eisenhower
> Supreme Allied Commander

Every G.I. had been issued a $10,000 life insurance policy. There was an announcement that anyone who had not made out a will should go to the supply office to make one. Noah made Ann his beneficiary.

Noah and David boarded an LST and were transported across the channel to Utah beach in Normandy, arriving on June 8th, two days after D-day. Noah's spirits were lifted by the sight of the battleship Texas. It was like seeing an old friend, and seemed a good omen. The LST landed about fifty-five feet from shore. Noah and David walked down the ramp into eight feet of forty-five-degree water. They each had a combat medical pouch slung over their shoulder and extra bandages and other supplies stuffed into their shirts and jackets.

"Man, I thought I signed up as a ground-pounder, not a sailor. If Ike thinks this is such a noble crusade he needs to come over here and get his feet wet. We can go to his headquarters back in England." David complained, attempting to keep his head above water.

"You better keep your mouth closed and start swimming, or you'll end up as a submariner," replied Noah as he dog-paddled in the water.

They struggled at first, but finally managed to swim and wade to shore. Once there, everything was mass confusion. Military police were frantically trying to act as traffic cops. There were pieces of bloody clothing and discarded gear and equipment lying all around. Occasionally a German shell would land nearby. Noah and David made it to the top of the ridge and moved inland. After a long march the word came to "dig your foxhole." There were hedgerows which Noah chose to dig away from, fearing that they offered too much cover for Germans to hide behind. All that marching and digging really made Noah and David hungry. They were grateful when mess was called.

"Man, dig this hot grub," David said, rubbing his hands enthusiastically. "I think I've died and gone to heaven."

They were behind the mess truck when shots rang out from a copse of trees, killing one of the men in their company. Noah stood transfixed, staring at the body. It was the first casualty he had seen personally. David let his food slide from his plate. A jeep with a machine gun was brought up and sprayed the trees. Leaves and branches fell, along with a German sniper who was killed and left hanging in his harness. They dug in for the night to get some rest before making their push forward the next morning. Noah was exhausted and quickly fell asleep, but not before praying that Ann would be spared the violence he had just seen. The next morning, when Noah arose and left his foxhole, he realized that he had been sleeping about fifteen feet from an ammunition truck loaded with rounds for the artillery company's howitzers. He shuddered when he thought about what might have happened if a German shell had landed nearby.

Later that morning, the company was ordered to progress to St. Lo where they set up a dispensary-field station in an abandoned storefront. That afternoon, they encountered an intense exchange of artillery fire from both sides. Noah, joined by David, were running back and forth hugging the walls in search of safety, waiting until the fighting stopped.

"Watch out for yourself," Noah said to David.

"No need to worry! I got nine lives, just like a cat," David replied with bravado.

They had just sat down to rest for a moment when suddenly, out of nowhere, came an excruciating scream followed by voices yelling, "Medic, Medic!" Noah stood, transfixed, until David shook him, nodding toward the sound. They ran toward the voices and came upon a soldier who had been unlucky enough to have stepped on a land mine. His leg was blown off just above the knee. A group of soldiers were standing around, watching the wounded, blood-soaked man squirming on his back and flopping from side to side. Noah stared transfixed at the scene before him, but also knew he was expected to handle the situation. He was terrified and felt faint, not believing what he was seeing.

He was shocked out of his stupor by one of the men asking him in a loud voice, "What are you goanna do, Doc?" The man asked in grief and agitation.

Noah, saying a quick prayer to himself, dropped to his knees beside the moaning man. There was a massive amount of blood spurting out of an artery in the exposed thigh. Noah realized that it must be stopped, or the soldier would soon bleed to death. He pulled back the torn pants leg and placed his fist against the stub of the shattered limb. Then, after a brief interval, he ripped off a piece of the pants, tied it around the man's leg as a tourniquet. He instructed David to get a morphine kit from the medical pack, and then injected the pain killer into the man's abdomen while telling some of the men standing around to go find a litter.

The next part was the most difficult for Noah. He selected the largest needle and suture he could find in his kit and began sewing the jagged flesh shut, hoping to reach the retracted femoral artery. He continued sewing until he felt he had gathered enough flesh to help stem the bleeding. Finally, he covered the wounded area with sulfur powder and applied bandages; no easy feat since the remaining stump was slippery with blood.

Once satisfied that the bandages would hold, Noah removed the tourniquet, praying it had not been in place too long. The stretcher-bearers arrived as he finished and carried the soldier off. David, along with some of the other men, patted Noah on the back, congratulating him for a great job. He silently gave thanks to God for helping him through this battlefield coming of age. He instinctively knew that this was a turning point in his transformation into adulthood and his pursuit of a career in medicine. Noah realized at that moment that he had a God-given ability. He hoped someday to put this to use in helping the people in his beloved Fairview. He only wished he could share his revelation with Ann.

A few days later Noah was working in the infirmary when he saw or rather smelled, David.

"What happened to you?" Noah asked.

"I was out in this pasture where there were a lot of dead, bloated cows, when the Germans began to shell. One landed near the carcasses and the shrapnel punctured them. You could hear the cows exploding like balloons. Some of the debris landed on me. Man, they stunk! I could hardly breathe!" David said holding his noise.

"You're not the only one who can't breathe!" Noah said, fanning the air in front of his face. You'd better clean up fast. I hear we're going to move out soon."

"Ah man, I'd like to, but I've got a bone in my leg," David said, rubbing his leg.

Noah laughed, then slapped David on the head and told him to get going.

The next day they headed out. The Air Force had begun a bombing campaign to soften up the area where they were headed. Noah spent some time tending to German prisoners. A few of them were injured, but most were suffering from shell shock and bleeding from their ears from concussion. They gestured or asked in broken English for a cigarette. Even though Noah did not smoke he obliged, seeing in these shivering, shaken, prisoners' men like himself who, if given the choice, would just as soon be at home with their loved ones.

Noah was called to a spot where a German 88 shell had landed. There he found six bodies fanned out on the ground. At first, he thought they were all dead, but on closer inspection found that the shell had landed in the middle of them and the shrapnel had apparently gone over their heads. They all had been knocked unconscious by the force of the explosion but were alive. He was amazed at seeing this and thought these men must all have nine lives, just like David.

CHAPTER 20

Over the next few days, Noah and David treated many men suffering numerous types of injuries. One call came from a tank battalion seeking help for some of their wounded men. When they arrived, Noah was surprised to find that the men were colored. He learned they were members of the 761st, an all Negro command.

He treated the most serious one first, a young man with a gaping hole in his leg. He refused an injection of morphine, telling Noah, "Just patch me up doc. I got to get going and I want to stay alert."

Noah was impressed with the bravery and dedication of this man, but, remembering Sam, he was not surprised. He had read about a Lieutenant Jackie Robinson, a baseball player in the Negro league who was court-martialed for refusing to sit at the back of a civilian bus going from Fort Hood, Texas where he was stationed, to the nearby town of Belton. He was eventually acquitted and Noah took great pleasure in reading years later that Jackie Robinson was riding on buses in the major league after breaking baseball's color barrier.

Noah talked to several of the men and one showed him a message that had been issued from Lt. General, George S. Patton, Jr.:

"Men, you are the first Negro tankers to ever fight in the American Army. I would never have asked for you if you were not good. I have nothing but the best in my Army. I do not care what color you are as long as you go up there and kill those Kraut sons of bitches. Everyone has their eyes on you and is expecting great things from you. Most of all, your race is looking forward to you. Do not let them down and damn you do not let me down."

One of the men told Noah that the soldier he had patched up was their platoon sergeant who had been told on his radio by an officer, "Don't go into that town, Sergeant, it's too hot in there." The sergeant had respectfully replied, "I'm sorry, sir, I'm already through that town."

Noah and David had been operating under a false sense of security that they would not be fired upon while wearing their Red Cross armbands and having it painted on their helmets. They were retrieving an injured soldier when sniper fire began; near enough, but fortunately missing them. When they got back to the aid station, David went to fill his canteen.

"Son-of-a-Bitch." he muttered, watching the water flow out of a bullet hole in his canteen.

"Looks like you used up one of your nine lives," Noah said. "So I guess you better start being more careful, seeing as you only have eight left."

The next day they were enjoying the warmth of the Battalion aid station that was set-up in what had been a beer hall. The owner still had a few kegs that he happily tapped for the boys to enjoy. There was still shelling going on but they felt much safer inside. This idyllic set-up was soon interrupted by the cry of, "Medic!"

"Damn, I knew it was too good to be true," David said, finishing off the last of his stein's contents of beer.

"Come on, let's go!" Noah said, disquieted by the soldiers cry for help.

They soon learned that a tank commander had been wounded and was 500 or so yards away, across sniper infested territory, at the other end of town. Noah and David were called to his aid. A cold drizzle was falling as they threaded their way through the mortar-torn streets, staying close to the buildings for protection. About a block from their destination, they were spotted and the enemy opened fire on them. They safely made the last block in one quick dash. As they were patching up the commander, mortars began falling around them. It was decided that the safest way to move the commander was to put him inside the relative safety of the tank. Noah and David lowered him through the turret and the hatch was quickly slammed shut. There was not room enough for all of them so Noah and David were forced to return on foot. Choosing to take a different route on the return trip, they had gone only a short distance when they encountered enemy fire.

"Keep low!" Noah hollered to David.

"Don't worry about me. I'm like a cat, remember? I got nine lives." Then remembering the incident with the canteen, added, "Well I guess I used up one of them, but I've still got eight more. You just watch out for yourself." David said.

They ducked into the first building they could, which turned out to be a fortuitous choice for them since it was a home for the aged and run by an order of Nuns. As soon as the Sisters found out that Noah and David were Americans, nothing was too good for them. The nuns brought clothes to warm them while they cleaned and dried their uniforms. The best was yet to come: they were led to a table and treated to a feast of fresh baked bread, cheese, and fruit, along with several bottles of excellent wine. This small bit of civility and sanity created images of home and Ann that tugged at Noah's heart.

"We better get back," Noah said, thankful for the respite.

"I think we owe it to these kind Sisters to stay here and protect them," David suggested, smiling sheepishly.

Noah laughed but insisted they needed to get going. They changed back into their uniforms, thanked the nuns, and started off again, heading for the river that ran through town. The river was waist deep, cold, and fairly swift, but they crossed safely, except that once again they were soaking wet and cold.

"Shit," David said, wiping the mud from his boots. "Just as I was enjoying being warm and dry."

The following day, Noah was out in the combat area when he saw an officer of whom he needed to ask a question.

"Lieutenant Cross!" Noah cried out.

"You know better than to address me like that out here!" the Lieutenant replied.

"But I did call you Lieutenant, sir," Noah replied, thinking he was referring to a lack of respect.

"Shh, no, don't call me Lieutenant out here." He said angrily. Noah realized what he was saying, remembering how David had narrowly missed being one of a number of medics that had been killed or wounded by Germans, who did not respect the Red Cross emblem that American medics wore on their sleeve and helmet.

Later, a directive came out explaining that snipers were on the lookout for officers and high ranking non-commissioned officers. As a consequence, officers should avoid salutes and remove their rank from their uniforms.

The town was finally secured and Noah's division was assigned to General Patton's Third Army. They were going to give the Germans a taste of blitzkrieg, American style. The orders were to keep moving forward in swift attacks, disrupting German supply lines until all the gas in their vehicles was expended and that is what they did, coming to a halt near Verdun and the Meuse. All along the way they kept seeing signs that read, Kilroy was here.

"Man, that 'Kilroy' must be one bad son-of-a-bitch," David exclaimed.

As they crossed France, they received enthusiastic greetings from the French civilian population. People would line the streets in the small villages, wave American flags, and call out to vehicles that had names on them.

"Vive la Mary!"

"Vive la Betty!"

"Vive la Susan!"

When Noah and David went by, there was a Prestone 44 antifreeze container on the side of their jeep. Suddenly a cheer went up.

"Vive la Prestone!" The crowd shouted.

They would yell out, "You've done it again!" Noah wondered what they had done again, until he was told the U.S. Army had liberated this village during World War I.

They bivouacked in the town. That evening David decided to check out the local women and tried to talk Noah into going with him, saying, "A little strange stuff would do you good. I got all this money they pay me and it's burning a hole in my pocket. I'm going to spend some on women, some on whiskey, and I'll just waste the rest of it."

Noah declined, making up a lame excuse about not feeling well, but in fact all he could think about was Ann. The next day David sought out Noah.

"Hey, what's going on?" Noah asked him.

"Man, I itch," David said, as he scratched his pubic area. "I think I got something wrong."

They went to the infirmary where an older doctor looked at him.

"Son, you've got body lice," the doctor told him. David looked at him incredulously "Crabs," the doctor explained. "Don't worry, they're easy to get rid of, but you need a toothpick, lighter fluid, and a razor. What you do is shave the hair off on one side of your crotch, then pour the lighter fluid on the remaining side with hair on it and set it on fire. When they start running across you stab them with the toothpick," the doctor said, maintaining a straight face. David just stared at him, dumbfounded.

The doctor laughed, handing David a tube of ointment, "Keep applying the ointment, wear clean clothes, and make sure not to share clothing or bedding with anyone else," he instructed.

For days afterwards, his buddies would hold out their Zippo lighters and ask him if he would like to borrow them.

One evening Noah and David were sitting around a campfire with a group of soldiers exchanging war stories. It had been raining, as usual, and they were sitting on their helmets to avoid the mud.

"Man, this is a fucked-up way to spend an evening, having to sit on your piss-pot just to keep your butt dry." David grumbled.

"Quit complaining,'" one of the men said. "At least you have a butt to try and keep dry." They talked of seeing men who had their legs blown off from stepping on a pencil mine. One told of seeing his buddy's head blown off and another of trying to stuff his friend's guts back inside him after he had been opened up by shrapnel. There was a report of finding dead horses with pieces of flesh missing where starving people had cut them up for meat. One told a story of entering a village behind a tank and coming under sniper fire. The shots were coming from a building where a woman was standing, holding a baby. The tank trained its turret on the doorway, and blew it all away, including the woman and her baby.

"Why?" Noah asked, feeling such remorse.

"It was the direction the shooting came from," was the callous reply.

Noah thought how that could have been Ann in the doorway, and prayed that the war would soon be over and Ann would soon be safe once more in his arms.

One of the men told how he had seen German prisoners lined up and an American soldier opened fire on them with his machine gun. When his buddies tried to stop him he said he was just getting revenge for his friend who had been shot by the Germans.

Noah realized that so called "civilized" men were rapidly degenerating into their base animal instincts. God, how he hated this war and longed to be back in Fairview, with Ann and the people he loved.

Thanksgiving came, along with more rain and for the first time in weeks, a hot meal. The mess truck provided hot turkey, mashed potatoes, peas and carrots, fruit cocktail, cookies, and hard candies. Noah and David sat in their ponchos, on a pile of straw and manure, in the rain, and still gave thanks for this temporary respite. They lived from day to day and sometimes from hour to hour, surrounded by the death and destruction that this war produced. They received their mail, reading it under their ponchos to keep it dry.

"Shit!" David exclaimed.

"What's the matter?" Noah asked.

"Jo Lynn's gotten married, to a sailor!" he said in disgust.

Noah stared at the envelope he received, studying it before he opened it, praying that it would be from Ann. It was not to be; but was just a letter from his mother filled with small talk about home.

> Dear Noah,
>
> I hope you are safe and doing well. The war is causing a lot of hardships and disruptions. Rationing has been in force and such things as gas, tires, sugar, butter, coffee, meat, even shoes, are strictly limited. Each family receives a ration book and has to buy based on a point system. Now that they have rationed cigarettes and nylons, I think I might shoot Hitler myself.
>
> We have joined a neighborhood victory garden and are even raising chickens for meat and eggs. Michael is mad because now that gas rationing is in effect, he can no longer drive the truck to deliver groceries. Instead he has to use his old bicycle. I want you to know how proud I am to be a Blue Star mother. I have your Blue Star in the front window, so everyone will know I have a son who is fighting for them. It is so sad when I see a Gold star displayed. I feel so sorry for that family's loss.
>
> Please be careful so we don't have to change our star. Your grandparents are well and send their love. Michael says to tell you to forget about the Lugar and just take care of yourself. Dad sends his love. Tell David hello from all of us.
>
> Love,
> Mother

Noah felt both longing, and at the same time, comfort in reading about life at home. He noticed that his Mother still made no reference to Ann.

One of the men had a radio tuned to a broadcast of Axis Sally. They enjoyed the large inventory of popular American music she played and her sultry voice.

"Hi fellows, this is Gerry's Front calling with the tunes that you like to hear and a warm welcome from radio Berlin. I'm afraid you would like to hear the voice of someone else, but I just wonder if she isn't running around with the 4-Fs back home. Well, here is something to take your mind off of that."

"Way to go Sally. Man, you really know how to get to a guy, bringing up those stinking 4-Fs," David retorted. "I'm sick to death hearing that German bitch."

Noah listened as she played Vera Lynn singing, 'We'll meet again,' followed by Frank Sinatra's recording of 'I'll be seeing you', and 'I'll be home for Christmas.' He finally had to walk away, not being able to listen to anymore.

Their reprieve was not long-lived. The next day they were on their way again.

CHAPTER 21

Patton's 3rd army was moving along at a good clip towards Germany when the massage came that Bastogne in Belgium was under siege by a large German force and needed help. Old "Blood and Guts" Patton did not hesitate and turned sharply around and headed to their aid.

They arrived the day after Christmas in unbelievably cold weather. The air was so cold and still you could literally hear the proverbial pin drop and ice crystals hung suspended in the frozen air. It was so cold that it could not even snow. Thank God. There was already enough snow on the ground. If it was another place, another time, it might have been beautiful, but there was nothing beautiful about this place. Everywhere Noah looked there were burned out German tanks, vehicles, and dozens of dead bodies, both German and American.

Noah was thankful that because of the cold, he could not smell the rotting flesh. That was something he could not get used to. He had never been so cold in his life, but somehow, he had to help those men who were still alive. There were many wounded but they were finding more and more men out in the field, usually in their foxholes, with severe frostbite. Most of the men could not walk and had to be carried back to the field station on the backs of the medics.

Noah and David went to the area set aside to serve as a field hospital. There they met a medic named Mark.

"Boy am I glad to see you guys," Mark said, "Best Christmas present I've ever received."

"Yeah, glad we can help." Noah said.

"Man, it's colder than a witches' tit in a brass bra." David said, hugging himself.

"Yeah or a well diggers ass in Nome Alaska." Mark said with a laugh.

"One things for sure, I'm not going to complain about it around General P." David said. "I heard how he slapped those two soldiers in that hospital in Sicily for what he thought was cowardice. He probably would shoot us." David finished with a laugh.

Noah shook his head and asked "How can we help?" Then both he and David took off their packs full of supplies.

"Thanks, we were about out of all our supplies." Mark said.

"Let's get to work." Noah said.

They worked for a number of hours and then stopped for some coffee that they had brought in with them.

"Man, this sure tastes good. We've been out for days," Mark said. "Did you guys hear about what happened when the German commander asked our commander, General McAuliffe to surrender?"

Both Noah and David shook their heads "No."

"Well the word is he told that Kraut commander, 'Nuts,' Mark laughed.

"I noticed that there seems to be a good number of Negro soldiers here." Noah said.

"Yes, they are the 333rd African American Army field artillery battalion; they were stationed here. I have to say they fight like hell." Mark said.

Later Noah was to find out that the 333rd was awarded a Presidential Unit citation for their heroism.

They had fought through the Battle of the Bulge and liberated Bastogne. David was in awe of Patton and boasted that, "Old blood and guts will get the job done." Noah thought it amusing that members of the 101st Airborne kept insisting that they didn't need to be rescued.

Several weeks later they had come to this place, a small crossroads and railroad center. Noah thought it sad that this town was completely destroyed. He could see here and there that once there must have been beautiful houses and neat little cottages with a town center and small square with a statue in the middle of the square. Who knew what the statue had been; it was all just a heap of rubble now.

The only structure that was still partly standing was the bombed-out railway station alongside the railroad tracks. That is, where the rails had been. Most of them had been torn up and used by the Germans to make more arms. There were a few cattle cars on a siding off to one side. Noah, David, and the other medics set up an aid station in the station ruins and moved the wounded men inside. It was not weatherproof, but was warmer than sleeping outside.

A number of troops that were outside decided to sleep inside the cattle cars even without heat, with the men in such close quarters, it was better than the bone chilling cold outside. Exhausted from days of fighting and miles of marching in bitter cold, the troops bedded down and were soon in deep sleep.

At first light, Noah and David tended the men. Most were holding their own and it seemed as if the war was a thousand miles away. "Maybe with a few more nights like this we'll be able to get a lot of these men recuperated and out of here," Noah said, as he dressed the frost-bitten foot of one of the men. "Wish we could all get out of here," he thought to himself.

Suddenly Noah heard the unmistakable whining sound of German Stukas and felt sick in the pit of his stomach. The two airplanes seemed to come out of nowhere, screaming down from the sky. They dropped their few bombs, and then made several low passes over the area, firing their machine guns. The Americans, though taken by surprise, had rallied and were returning fire. The deafening thud of "ack-ack" was all that could be heard.

After about ten minutes they were gone. Now that the guns were silent, Noah and David could hear the screams of pain and panic coming from the cattle cars. What had started out as a haven from the cold had become a coffin. One had been hit by a bomb and the smoking wreckage, along with the human wreckage, lay scattered on the ground. All the cars had been hit by machine gun fire.

"Oh, my God!" was all Noah could say as he and David ran to the cars. Men who had been able to climb out of the cars were wandering around aimlessly, wounded and dazed. The cars were awash in blood and bodies as Noah climbed inside. It was all he could do to keep from vomiting. He couldn't help thinking that this must be what Hell looks like.

After several minutes of chaos, the walking-wounded were ordered to fall in. Anyone who was able would man the guns and help tend the wounded. Noah functioned with an efficiency that bordered on robotic. Noah looked with horror at the scene before him - with so many young men dead, dying, disfigured, and maimed. It was almost more than he could stand. How, he wondered, could men do this to each other and how could God allow it? For the first time since his arrival, he wondered how much more he could endure. He said a prayer, asking for, understanding, or if not, at least strength to carry on.

It was late March of 1945 when Gen. Patton's Third Army began its famous bridging and crossing operation of the Rhine river into Germany. Without the luck of the 9th Armored Division who were able to capture the only intact bridge across the Rhine, Patton faced the necessity of bridging the wide river with their own resources. There had been a total of 22 road and 25 railroad bridges spanning the Rhine into Germany.

Patton made the following statement to his men; "You have taken over 6,400 square miles of territory, seized over 3,000 cities, towns and villages including Trier, Koblenz, Bingen, Worms, Mainz, Kaiserslautern, and Ludwigshafen. You have captured over 140,000 soldiers, killed or wounded an additional 100,000 while eliminating the German 1st and 7th Armies. Using speed and audacity on the ground with support from peerless fighter-bombers in the air, you kept up a relentless round-the-clock attack on the enemy. Your assault over the Rhine at 2200 last night assures you of even greater glory to come."

During the crossing some 154-enemy aircraft had attacked in an attempt to dislodge the foothold on the west bank but effective anti-aircraft fire brought down a number of them and there was little damage. One thing that was not known until later was that several of the attacking planes were the first jet aircraft the German Me 262. They heckled the operation all day but their speed and apparently inexperienced pilots resulted in only one hit with little damage.

When Noah and David crossed over into Germany David fell to his knees and kissed the earth; Noah just looked up and gave a silent thanks to God.

A few days later, the company was on the move and marching single file down a narrow road. A German sniper opened fire. The men scrambled for cover behind a rock fence. David poked his head over the wall to see if he could tell where the shots were coming from. There was a shot and David fell back. Noah rushed to his side. "No, no!" Noah cried.

"Relax, still got seven lives left, remember? I'm okay, but this piss-pot isn't," David said, holding up his helmet with a jagged tear on the side. "That's the second time they've shot up my gear. I hope the quartermaster doesn't try to collect from me."

"Another two inches and it would have been between your eyes! That hollow head of yours would have exploded like a balloon," Noah said, relieved to see David spared.

The men decided it would be best to leave the sniper to the infantry so they moved down to a dry river bed in order to make their way around the action. Just as they reached the river bed,

Noah realized that in the confusion, he had left his medical kit up by the road.

"Leave it," David said.

"We might need it," Noah responded.

"Watch yourself then," David warned, as Noah skittered back up the hill.

"I will," Noah said over his shoulder, as he crawled away. Noah cautiously made his way back up the slope to the rock fence and retrieved the kit. He was relieved to have found it and began sliding back down the hill to the riverbed where the rest of the men were waiting. David waved to Noah to hurry up. Suddenly an artillery shell exploded nearby, followed quickly by another that landed even closer. Noah was blown into the air several feet. When the smoke and dust cleared, he saw the hell below. The second shell had landed in the middle of the men waiting in the riverbed below. Noah could not speak, he just ran to the carnage. He looked around in stunned disbelief. Some of the men were obviously dead; several had body parts missing and lay moaning.

At first, he could not see David, but then he spotted him at the edge of the group and rushed to where he lay. David was lying motionless, covered with dirt and debris. Noah remembered his experience with a German '88 at St. Lo and how it had only stunned a group of men. Noah hoped and prayed that David was only stunned but as he knelt down beside him, he saw an ominous stain of blood creeping out from under David's body. He pulled David up to a seated position, forgetting in his anxiety that it was the wrong thing to do.

"Man, that was something," David said, and then coughed. Noah noticed the frothy blood that came forth. He felt the sticky wetness on his hands as he cradled David.

"Don't talk. I'll get you to the aid station," Noah told him shakily, trying not to let on to David how bad it looked.

"Thanks, but I don't think it'll do any good. Just stay here with me," David whispered as he gripped Noah's hand. "Looks like I used up my nine lives. I'm sorry I won't be around to take care of you and I won't be there when you find Ann. I sure would like to ask her what she sees in an ugly S.O.B. like you," David said, trying to laugh, but choking on his blood. Noah could barely see through his tears but would not relinquish his hold to wipe them away. Suddenly, David convulsed, and then was still.

"No God! No!" Noah wailed in a plaintiff voice almost lost in his sobs.

Noah became an automaton, functioning with his body while trying not to let thoughts and feelings creep through. He wrote to David's parents, telling them about his death and how sorry he was. He wrote his parents and grandparents, letting them know he was okay and telling them how much he missed them and home. He was sick of war; of the death, of the destruction, and of man's insanity and inhumanity. He wanted it over. Most of all he wanted the loving, comfort, warmth, and companionship of Ann. It was the thought of her that kept him going.

Sometimes when searching a deserted house, he would come across wine that someone had left in their haste to get away. He'd take a bottle, and at night would find solace from his surroundings and sorrows in its contents. One night he had an overpowering thirst and no remedy. He remembered that the aid station had 180 proof grain alcohol that could be mixed with the canned juice that was available. He sneaked in, found a bottle, poured the contents in a glass, and then added the juice. He had just finished drinking it when a lieutenant walked in and asked what he was doing. "Nothing, just having a drink. Too bad there's no juice left." Noah could care less about the consequences. Holding the glass in a cavalier manner, Noah asked the lieutenant if he wanted to join him.

The lieutenant picked up the glass, smelling its contents, and then looked around. Seeing the source, he yelled, "You fool, that's rubbing alcohol. It will kill you. Here drink this," He handed Noah a bottle of Syrup of Ipecac and then escorted him outside. "Now stick your finger as far as you can down your throat." Noah followed his instructions and started to vomit. The Lieutenant handed him a canteen full of water along with a handful of charcoal tablets, "Take all of those and drink all of the water," he said. After that experience, Noah gave up drinking, but the void he felt was always there.

As Patton's army rolled its way across Germany, Noah found little time for morose feelings since there was no shortage of wounded, both allied and German, to keep him busy. Urban fighting and resistance at times was fierce, but the Germans had wasted their best men and resources defending the "Fatherland," and the war was over, for all practical purposes, before the Rhine had been crossed.

In one mop up operation, a group of soldiers were moving from house to house cleaning out pockets of resistance, when a German sniper shot one of the men. Noah saw it happen and rushed to where the solder had fallen and was too busy and excited to be aware of the continuing fire. He worked feverishly on his patient as the shooting continued. Suddenly he felt sharp pain as a bullet hit him in the flesh of his thigh. Noah kept working, despite the pain, until he had the soldier stabilized. Several soldiers told him afterwards that they had shot the sniper.

Later, when he saw the sniper's body, he was aghast to see a young boy who could not have been more than fourteen. Tears welled up in his eyes as he thought of Michael. He could not help feeling sorry, not only for this young German, but for the incredible waste of young lives this war had created.

Noah's wound was minor and only required treatment at the aid station. When he learned he was to receive a Purple Heart and the Distinguished Service Cross for his disregard of his personal safety in pursuing his duty, he vowed to himself, that if he made it home, he would throw both away in the trash.

The Ruhr pocket was eliminated and it was then that the troops learned of President Roosevelt's death. It was a sad day for everyone and though he was emotionally drained and numb to death, Noah still felt sadness for the man and the country.

Over the next three weeks, Noah's unit pushed over 200 miles to the Elbe River, only 50 miles from Berlin. They linked up with the Russians and exchanged cigarettes and vodka. His unit could have easily taken the city, but for political reasons, the honor was given to the Russians. Noah was shocked to see Russian women wearing the same uniform as the men and carrying the same weapons. Upon further inquiry, he was told that the women were more ruthless than the men.

One day while waiting to move forward, Noah heard someone calling his name. He turned around and saw Ted Martin, the soda jerk from Ira's drugstore, striding toward him.

"Hey Noah! Boy, it sure is good to see a face from home," Ted said, giving him a hug.

"Of all the gin joints in all the world," Noah said, paraphrasing a line from the movie Casablanca he had recently seen, thanks to the USO.

"How's Ann?" Ted asked.

"I don't know. She never returned from Paris. I received several letters and then they stopped. I just pray she's all right," Noah said, anxiously.

"I'm sure she is. She probably has gotten caught up in the war. Since Paris is liberated I'm sure she's safe and just hasn't been able to get in touch," Ted said, reassuringly.

They talked about the war and shared news from home. "I've decided to go into the ministry." Ted told Noah. Maybe I can help turn hate into love, and help shape a new generation."

Noah told him about David, trying hard to hold back his tears. "I hope you'll use your ministry to turn all this hate and senseless killing into peace and love," Noah sobbed in anger and depression

"I hope so too. I'm sorry to hear about your friend. How about you? What are you going to do after this is over?" Ted asked.

"I want to find Ann then finish medical school and take over my grandfather's practice." Noah said.

"I think Fairview will be lucky to have you. There's a lot of your grandfather's compassion in you. I know it will all turn out okay. I'll keep both you and Ann in my prayers." Ted said.

"Thanks, Ted. You might add all of us and this insanity to that prayer," Noah responded.

Victory in Europe was announced; however, even though the war was over in Europe, it was not in the Pacific. Noah's unit was granted leave, but not allowed to go home. After some rest they were to regroup and retrain for the invasion of Japan. Noah and his comrades were in the midst of celebrating when they received orders to join the Third Calvary in administering medical care to a concentration camp on the Danube River in Austria. Noah could not believe what he saw when he arrived. It seemed eerily strange, the cruel contrast between the idyllic natural beauty of the picturesque Austrian lake town and the horror of the human evils that took place in its shadows.

The camp at Ebensee held Jews, Russians, and political prisoners. Noah had heard rumors about these camps and had once overheard an officer talking about the atrocities he had seen at the camp at Bergen Belsen. Noah thought the man must have exaggerated, but now realized he did not. He had become somewhat accustomed to the sight of illness, suffering, and death, but the magnitude and brutality of this was beyond belief. He felt physically sick as he saw men who had once been doctors, lawyers, professors, and businessmen reduced to walking skeletons with their bones sticking out of their bent, twisted, and shrunken bodies. Years of disease, torture, and malnutrition had taken a terrible toll on them. They had horribly diseased skin, huge running sores, areas where bone was exposed and discharging puss. More than once Noah became sick to his stomach as he watched men die by the dozens while he made his rounds. He witnessed five men drop dead while waiting in line for their first meal.

After several days of trying to restore the survivors to health, Noah was both physically and mentally exhausted. Allied forces worked steadily to bring water and sanitary facilities to the camp and set up delousing stations. They were faced with shortages of the basics such as clean clothing, blankets, and medical supplies. Captured German supplies were brought in. The former prisoners' barracks were emptied, fumigated, and scrubbed, and all of the old clothing and blankets burned. Patients with typhus, tuberculosis, and other infectious diseases were isolated and the others were categorized by their needs. It amounted to trying to run a city in which all the inhabitants were in the last stages of starvation, most of whom had one or more horrible disease, and where there was no basic sanitation, housing, clothing, or food.

Finally, U.S. Army commanders ordered the Germans and Austrians of the district be put to work in the camps, cleaning up the filth and washing the bedridden former prisoners. This was done not only to help alleviate the labor shortage, but also to make them experience firsthand the horrible truth about the regime they had supported. In addition, they were pressed into service to load and transport hundreds of corpses from the camp on carts through the main street, to the outskirts of town, where they were made to dig individual graves in an area marked by a sign that read in German, German Atrocity Cemetery.

Noah, his time in hell finally over, was given a leave. After making some quick arrangements, he immediately headed for Paris. He prayed that his search would be successful and soon he would once again hold his loving Ann in his arms. The anticipation of that was almost killing him. Thoughts of her were the only thing keeping him going through all the hell he had seen and been through.

CHAPTER 22

Noah was up early, eager to hop the next military flight out to Paris. He was eager to get started and did not want to waste time. It was already a bright, sunny, spring, Parisian day as he set out, determined to try to locate Ann. He requisitioned a jeep and went in search of the address he had for where Ann lived. He had little trouble finding the house, which sat on a quiet, tree-lined boulevard, nestled among similar homes, all in a neat row. Noah could see the Eiffel Tower in the distance and marveled at how Paris had avoided the destruction evident throughout the rest of Europe. It was encouraging to see "The City of Light,' as Ann had often referred to it. Noah parked the jeep, went up the steps, and, with a feeling of trepidation, knocked on the door, saying a silent prayer that Ann might answer. The door opened and a woman appeared whom Noah did not recognize. She resembled Ann, but seemed older and haggard.

"Hello, I'm Noah, Ann's husband," he said.

"Yes, I know. I'm Rachael. Please won't you come in?" she said, gesturing to the interior.

"Thank you," Noah replied, following her in, trying not to show his disbelief that this worn creature could be Ann's younger sister. He looked around, taking notice of the sparse furnishings. Rachael saw his interest.

"Most of the things disappeared when we left," she explained.

Noah wondered what she meant but decided to keep quiet.

"We have some chairs in the parlor," she said, motioning to a room off of the hall.

Noah could tell that this was once a very fine home. He followed Rachael and she invited him to sit down. She went to a table on which sat several bottles of wine, selecting two glasses, she filled them, and brought them back to where he was seated. Noah thanked her and took a sip.

"Thanks, I came to find Ann. Where is she?" Noah asked.

"I know why you are here. I have been expecting a call. I---" Rachael said hesitantly.

"Please, just tell me about Ann," Noah interrupted.

"I will Noah but let me start from the beginning. I think you need to know the whole story." Noah started to protest, but Rachel stopped him. "Please, I need to; for you, for Ann," she hesitated, "and for me. Please."

Noah nodded his acquiescence, trying to hide his impatience.

Rachael took a deep breath followed by a swallow of wine and began. "Noah, Ann thought about you and about going back to America constantly. She tried everything, even taking a job at a bookstore to save money, but it was impossible. Any way out of the country was either blocked or unbelievably expensive. There was no way to get help from outside. When France fell and the Germans marched into the city an armistice was signed, and France was divided into two zones, three fifths under German rule and the rest, to the South at Vichy, under a puppet government. Laws were passed. All Jews were required to wear a patch with a yellow Star of David. General DeGaulle set up an exile government in England and called for resistance. In November, there was a large student demonstration at the L'Arc de Triomphe to lay flowers at the tomb of the Unknown Solider. I told Ann I was going. She tried to talk me out of it, but I insisted, so she said she was going with me.

There was a large crowd milling about and the Germans had set up machine guns around the perimeter. Suddenly, without warning, they started firing low into the crowd to disperse them. Some people were killed, many were injured and arrested. We saw a Jewish boy we knew with his hands in the air and a pistol to his neck. We knew we would never see him again. We made it back home, but Ann was terribly upset by this and other events. Over the next few days, she decided she had to do something."

Rachael looked at Noah, smiled, and continued. "She knew that you would understand. A few weeks later, she was introduced by a friend to a young man who had parachuted into France from England. He was coordinating clandestine air operations for the Resistance and the Bureau d'Operations Aeriennes. He enlisted Ann to help in code work; translating field notes; giving coordinates for locations cleared for parachute and plane landings. She delivered the reports to radio operators who would transmit them to London. She was very excited to be doing something that she thought might shorten the war and then she would be able to come back to you sooner.

Part of her job was to find lodging for agents parachuting in from London. She had to use her real name when signing the leases to ward off suspicion. Ann knew that the arrest of any one of those agents would lead the Gestapo to her.

It finally became too risky to continue and she was told to stop but it was already too late. One landlord became suspicious. Hoping for a reward, he contacted the authorities and the Gestapo raided the apartment. When they found Ann's name on the lease and came to arrest her, one of the apartment residents called and tipped her off. She fled, thinking they would only arrest her. When the Gestapo arrived and discovered Ann gone, they arrested mother and me. The next day they caught Ann at the Gare du Nord train station and arrested her too."

Rachael paused and poured them another glass of wine.

"We were all taken to the La Santé prison, although mother and I did not know until later that Ann was also there. She was transferred to Fresnes prison outside Paris where she was placed in solitary confinement for several months. She told me that she spent the time talking to you and dreaming of what life would be like when the two of you were together again."

Trying in vain to control his emotions, Noah let out a sob.

"Should I continue or would you like for me to stop for a while?" Rachael asked, placing her hand on his shoulder.

"No, no please keep going." Noah said, with a sense of foreboding.

"We were all deported to Romainville, a transit camp where female prisoners were sent prior to deportation. It was there that we were reunited. Ann was devastated when she learned we had been arrested and she blamed herself. I think that hurt her more than being confined. Mother and I tried to assure her that it was just a matter of time because we were targeted Jews, and not to feel guilty. At least we were all together." Said Rachael, as she paused for another sip of wine.

A few weeks later they sent us, along with many other women, to Ravensbruck, north of Berlin. It was a camp designed to hold six thousand, but contained over eighty thousand near the end of the war. It was there we learned that we had been labeled NN, a designation for political prisoners who were supposed to disappear in the night and fog, never to be heard from again."

She paused, studied her hands, and then looked at Noah, "A lot of bad things happened there, things I cannot tell you. They are too personal."

Noah nodded, gesturing his understanding with his hand, trying to hold back thoughts of what he had witnessed at Ebensee.

Rachael got up, walked to the window and looked out. After a moment she turned and came back. Sitting down, she finished the contents of her wine glass and filled it up again. She offered Noah another, but he refused.

"It's okay," he said.

Rachael swirled the contents of her glass, took a large swallow, and tried in vain to keep her emotions in check. Her eyes darted about as a soft sob escaped her lips. "No, I need to tell you the whole story, for my sake as well as yours." She said the last part in almost a whisper then took a deep breath and continued. "I was young and considered pretty, so I became a target for the SS guards' sexual advances. I was raped and abused many times and eventually became pregnant. They performed a so-called abortion on me. Because of that, I can never have children."

Her face took on a tortured expression. "That was probably for the best, because babies and young children were killed, sometimes in the arms of their mothers."

"I was very sick and Ann took care of me. She nursed me back to health, gave me her food, and hid me from the guards. There were unspeakable medical experiments done on the prisoners, mostly Poles and Gypsies. A crematorium was built and thousands of women and children were gassed and then cremated." She paused and took another swallow of wine.

"Mother was very ill and lost her will to live. She had never gotten over my father's death, and despite all our efforts, she died."

Rachael let out a sob and closed her eyes for a moment. After a few tense moments she opened them and continued. "They came and took her body and threw it on a cart, like trash, with a mound of others. Ann possessed a remarkable inner strength that kept me going. She said she had to if she was going to see you again. She even managed to hide the medallion you had given her by sewing it into her clothing. I often saw her take her garment and hold the spot where it was sewn to her heart. It seemed to give her the strength to keep going."

"Word came that Paris had been liberated and the camp commander ordered all NN prisoners to be transported to another camp. We were told by other prisoners to avoid the transports at all costs, that certain death awaited those who went. We hid, which wasn't hard to do with so many prisoners, and thus avoided the transports. The allies were getting closer to the camp and the Germans decided to move everyone further into Germany.

Several weeks later, we were all herded into trucks and wagons and forced to head west in a convoy. Along the way, several Allied planes appeared overhead and the convoy pulled off to the side of the road. In the confusion, a number of prisoners made a break for the nearby woods. Ann tried to get me to go but I wouldn't. I couldn't, Noah. I was scared and tired, just used up. I had no more fight. Ann said she had to go, she had to get back. Then she laughed and said, besides, she had a bottle of champagne waiting. She jumped out then took off running. She was almost to the woods when the guards began firing."

Rachael paused, standing, with her hand on her throat, she stared at Noah.

"I saw Ann go down. They shot her." She began to cry. "Noah, I'm so sorry," she said between sobs. "She should have lived. I should have been the one to die. She had so much to live for, so much to look forward to." Rachael began to cry uncontrollably.

Noah sat, transfixed, stunned into silence. His hand instinctively went to the claw on the lanyard around his neck. After what seemed like an eternity, he got up, and with tears in his eyes, went to Rachael, and embraced her, holding her while they both continued to cry. They remained that way until they were both emotionally exhausted. Finally, Noah asked Rachael if she was all right.

"Yes, yes, I'm all right, but what about you?" Rachael asked him.

Noah shrugged and shook his head, "I don't know. I guess so." He said in disbelief. He paused, looked out the window, and then back at Rachael. "No damn it, I'm not! I won't be for a long, long time, if ever." He said angrily.

Rachael looked at him. "Ann would want you to go on. She loved you so very much."

"I know. I'll try. But I don't know if I can," Noah said. "What about you?" He asked Rachael.

"I met someone who was in one of the Concentration camps. He understands what I've been through and knows I can never have children. We're going to be married and adopt some of the children that were left homeless." Rachael said.

Gathering in his emotions, he smiled and said, "I'm happy for you. Is there anything I can do for you? Do you need anything?"

"Thanks, but no, I'm okay. There's something I want to give you." She walked over to a box, opened it, and took out a packet and handed it to him. "These are the letters you wrote to Ann and the ones she wrote to you and could not mail. I know she would want you to have them."

Noah reached out, took the bundle of letters, then hugged her, said goodbye, and walked out the door.

The day suddenly seemed a lot darker and colder. He buttoned his collar up around his neck. He had suffered with the loss of David, but this was infinitely worse. He felt as if he too was dead. He looked back for the last time at the house, and then cursed the sky.

"Damn you God! Damn you!" He wailed, then turned and walked away.

CHAPTER 23

Noah could not accept the reality that Ann was gone. What he had hoped would be a joyful reunion now felt like hell. He was disconnected from everything around him and was barely able to function. To pass the time, he would walk aimlessly for hours. Once, as he walked near a pond, he saw an empty turtle shell lying in the grass. "That's me – all used up, empty and alone," he mused; as he wandered on.

When his leave was up he returned to his unit. While waiting for reassignment, he spent most of his time in his room reading Ann's letters over and over. He could not even cry his tears were dried up. Word came down that Japan had surrendered. The war was finally over, but he found little solace in it. His war was just beginning.

His orders came, informing him he was to be discharged and sent home on a ship. Ordinarily, he would have rejoiced at the news, but he felt only despair. He had nothing to go back to, nothing to look forward to. The big emptiness he felt was sometimes too much to bear.

Noah was sent to Camp Norfolk, popularly known as Camp Lucky Strike, in Rheims, France for processing out. While there, word came that General Patton had died from the injuries he had suffered in an automobile accident. "Even got you." He thought.

From the camp, he went to England, where he boarded the Queen Mary for New York. As the ship sailed into New York harbor everyone except Noah crowded onto the deck to see the Statue of Liberty and listen to a recording of Kate Smith singing "God Bless America."

"Yeah, God," Noah thought, "bless America, but not me."

Noah decided to make a detour on his way home. He got off the train in a town where an army buddy now lived. Borrowing his buddy's car and a hand saw, Noah drove to Fairview, arriving in the middle of the night. Noah drove directly to the park. He opened the trunk, took out the saw, and went to the wedding tree he and Ann had planted. Looking around to make sure he was not seen, cut it down. Noah felt that in some way, the finality of this act would do away with this reminder of their happy times together. Just as he finished the final cut, he felt a wet breath on his leg. He was startled for a moment then looking down he saw Beau standing there, his tail wagging.

"Hey boy, good to see you," he said, reaching down to rub behind his ears. "I bet you miss her as much as I do."

He wanted to see his grandparents, Sam, Thelma and the others, but knew he could not handle it right now. He told Beau to go home, walked back to the car and drove off, never looking back, wiping away the tears from his eyes.

Even though he had been home three weeks, at times it felt like three hours, or three days, or three years. He had no sensation of time or place. He only existed in a state he did not want or care for. He slept until early afternoon, then would get up, eat a bite of something, not caring what, and speak begrudgingly to whoever happened to be present. He would then go back to his room where, sleeping little, he stayed until the next day. Often, he would lie on his bed talking to Ann, and then break down into tears, asking "why?" Over and over he questioned what he and she had done to deserve this.

Finally, his mother had enough.

"Arthur, you have to do something. I simply cannot take any more of Noah's behavior. He looks like death warmed over, he stinks, his room stinks, and before long, the whole house will stink," she complained, emitting soft small sobs as she bit her knuckles, trying to keep control of her emotions.

"I know. You're right. I'll try to talk to him," Arthur said. He walked over to Noah's room and knocked.

"Go away," came Noah's muffled reply.

"I am going to talk to you whether you want to listen or not," Arthur said.

Perhaps it was the uncharacteristic assertiveness of his father's voice that got Noah's attention. Whatever it was it caused him to open the door. He glowered at his father, who ignored his look and entered the room.

"Look Noah, I know you're hurting. Ann was a wonderful woman whom we had all grown to love." Arthur said with compassion.

"Yeah, even Mom," Noah answered sarcastically.

"Yes, even your mother. She doesn't display affection easily, but I can assure you she grew to like Ann and was growing used to the idea of the two of you together. She wanted to tell you but couldn't figure out how. But it isn't your mother I'm concerned about, it's you. You can't go on like this. You can't hide from life. No matter how hard you try, it always catches up with you." He gestured around the room, "You owe it to yourself and if that's not enough, you owe it to Ann. She would be disappointed if she saw you like this," Arthur said fervently.

"Leave her out of it," Noah replied steely, through clenched teeth.

"No, I won't. She is inexplicably a part of who you are. She loved you and you need to honor that love," Arthur said.

"What do you want me to do?" Noah sighed.

"I want you to open the door to this mausoleum, clean it up and clean yourself up. I want you to find a direction for your life."

His father studied him for a moment then said, "Do you remember Mr. Murphy who was in charge of the suit department at Johnson's men's store?"

Noah shook his head yes. His father continued.

"I was in there several years ago around Easter because your mother insisted I buy a
new suit to wear to the Easter church service. I don't know if you knew this but Mr. Murphy had a glass eye as the result of an accident. It was a warm day and the store was crowded with shoppers. Mr. Murphy was waiting on a number of customers and was leaning over a revolving pant rack when evidently the heat was causing him to sweat and it loosened his glass eye which fell out onto the spinning rack. It was like the ball on a roulette wheel and it went rolling off across the floor. There was a matronly woman standing nearby who happened to look down just as the glass eye rolled by. She let out a shriek and collapsed. Several people came over to help her. Mr. Murphy ignored them as he walked over and retrieved his eye which he promptly wiped off, reinserted it, and then returned to the pant rack as if nothing had happened."

His Father looked at Noah. "What I am trying to say is that you need to have a goal and stay focused on it." Arthur thought for a moment and then added, "You can go and stay with your grandparents if you. . ."

"No! No, I won't, I can't!" he said explaining, "There are too many memories there. I just couldn't face it right now."

"I understand. You can work in the store with Michael and me," his father offered.

Noah shook his head, "I know. I appreciate that, but I need to do something that will help me forget---- no, I can't forget, I'll never forget, but maybe I can find a purpose. Something that Ann would be proud of." He paused for a moment, looking at his father. "I would like to go back and finish medical school. I can use my G.I. Bill and then go back to Fairview and take over for Grandfather. Ann and I had talked about doing that and I know she would approve. It would give me a goal, a reason to go on."

His father reached out, embracing Noah. "I'm proud of you son. You've grown up, and I can tell you this, Ann would be proud of you, too." He said.

Later that day his mother approached him. "Noah," she said.

"What do you want now?" he growled.

"I want to talk to you."

"About what?" he asked curtly.

"I was wrong about you and Ann," she said softly, wringing her hands.

Noah was caught by surprise, then started to speak, but his mother held up her hand to stop him.

"Let me finish, please. Like most mothers, I had certain dreams for you. I thought you would finish medical school, marry a local girl, have children and stay here. I realize that was my dream and not yours. I wanted what I thought was best for you, but I now know that it was wrong for me to try to live your life. I was selfish. I have no right to choose what you do or who you love. I admit I was disappointed when you married Ann, but now I see how much she meant to you and I am truly sorry for what happened. I only wish we could start over." She began to cry. "I love you Noah, and although it's too late, I love Ann too. Please, please, forgive me."

Noah was stunned by her confession. He remained quiet for a moment, then took her in his arms and kissed her on the forehead.

"Thank you, Mother. I guess we've all changed a lot. I love you, too," he said, trying valiantly to retain his composure.

In the weeks that followed, Noah seemed to awake from the dead. He applied and was accepted back to the medical school he had attended before the war. GIs, who had served in the medical corps and had finished their first two years of medical school, were automatically advanced to residency. He cut his hair, shaved his beard, cleaned his room, began helping around the house, and occasionally worked at the grocery store with his father and

Michael. Both his parents, however, had noticed that at times he would seem to "disappear", even in a room full of people. On several occasions, they passed his room and heard what sounded like conversation and sometimes, muffled sobs coming from behind his door.

"It will take a long, long time for him to heal. We will just have to be here for him when he needs us," Arthur said to Louise.

"Arthur, I know I haven't told you often enough, but these last few years with the war have made me realize how truly precious time and life are." She reached out and took his hand. "I love you. I'm sorry I have neglected to tell you that. I'm especially sorry that I haven't shown it." She put her arm around him and gave him a kiss.

"Welcome back, I love you too," Arthur smiled and squeezed her hand.

"I think I'll go fix dinner." Louise said.

"Let's not change things too quickly," he responded with a laugh.

Noah found solace by immersing himself in his studies, but there were still moments when the memories of Ann would creep into his thoughts and he would become despondent. He had to fight hard to maintain control. Sleep did not come easily. Often, he would wake up in the middle of the night covered in sweat from dreams of Ann, David, and the war. He hated to be around crowds and found comfort in solitude. He seemed to feel Ann's presence when he was alone. This overwhelming need for isolation spurred him to move into an apartment near the school. He never went out or interacted with the other students, which earned him the nickname "The Ghost". Often, he found himself talking to Ann, telling her how much he missed her and that he was doing this because he knew it was what she wanted and would be proud of him. He had the painting of the two of them on the wall and kept the bottle of champagne on his desk as if they were going to open it soon. The stack of letters sat by his bed and he would often reread them. He never took off his wedding band and would unconsciously fiddle with it and the claw necklace, thinking of Ann. The days came and went, filled with the routine of hospital rounds and studies. He went home for a few days at Christmas, but was glad to get back to the sanctuary of the school. While home, he ran into Ted Martin.

"Hey Noah," Ted called out.

"Hi Ted. What are you doing here?" Noah asked.

"I'm enrolled in seminary here, how about you?" Ted asked.

Noah told him about medical school and his continued commitment to return to Fairview.

"That's great. Say, what about Ann? Did you find her?" Ted asked.

Noah felt a momentary lump rise in his throat as he fought to hold back tears as he told him what he had found out.

"I'm so sorry Noah." Ted said.

"Yeah, it looks like God's got it in for me." Noah said with a sneer.

"What do you mean?" Ted asked.

"If there is a God and if he gave a shit, he wouldn't have let Ann and David die or allow all the suffering and destruction that happened. It was all so senseless."

"Noah, I'm so sorry, but you know it's not God's fault, it's ours." Ted said.

"What do you mean?" Noah asked incredulously.

"I believe God gives us free will. Life is a test. God wants us to do the right thing, but we screw it up on our own." Ted offered.

"Well I guess you have to believe that, since you are going into the ministry. Just don't expect me to buy into it." Noah said.

"I'll pray for you." Ted said.

"Don't waste your time. I don't think God, if he exists, gives a rat's ass about me, or Ann, or David. If he did, he wouldn't have let them die." Noah said adamantly.

"Give it time, Noah. You'll understand one of these days." Ted said.

"No, you're wrong, Ted. I will never understand," Noah said vehemently.

"You know, Noah, God doesn't give up on us. We give up on God." Ted said.

After talking awhile longer, they said goodbye.

Spring came, but even its beauty could not lift his spirits. It had been a year since he had learned of Ann's death. He immersed himself in his work, but even that had lost its meaning. He kept telling himself he owed it to Ann, but he was rapidly losing direction and it was becoming harder to stay focused. He found himself sitting at his desk, fingering the claw necklace and staring at the painting on the wall. In more lucid moments he realized he was about used up and soon would not be able to continue.

CHAPTER 24

One sunny spring morning, Noah was interrupted by a knock on his door. He did not like being disturbed and begrudgingly went to answer it. One of the other students was standing there.

"Yeah, what do you want?" he said curtly.

"There's someone to see you." The student answered.

"I'm busy. Tell them to leave their name and number and I'll call them." Noah said, knowing he would not.

"I was told to give you this." Holding out his hand, he revealed a medallion.

Noah stared at it, transfixed and disbelieving. Letting out a gasp, he pushed past the resident and, with a sense of trepidation, headed toward the lobby. He bounded down the stairs two at a time, and there, standing in the light streaming through the glass of the front door, stood a woman. The sunlight spilling through the door caused a halo effect and gave her a spectral glow. He was unable to see who she was. He started forwards and then recognition flooded over him and his breath caught in his throat. He stood in shocked silence for a moment, then raced to the figure and took her in his arms. It was Ann!

"How...where...?" He stuttered, crying and kissing her face.

She just shook her head and kissed him with a long, lingering kiss which he gratefully returned, dispelling all the years of longing and frustration. He realized, in that kiss, she was not a vision or figment of his imagination. At long last they broke apart and she reached out and took his hand.

"I'll tell you everything, but first we have a bottle of champagne to open." Ann said and kissed him again.

Walking hand in hand back to his room, Noah still could not believe this was happening. Gone was the young girl from that long-ago summer, instead replaced by a woman who had been through enough adversity for several lifetimes. Her face had acquired faint lines and there were streaks of gray in her now short hair. Yet to him she was even more beautiful in her maturity.

They spent the rest of the morning getting reacquainted. They chilled and drank the champagne, then spent the next few hours hugging, kissing and making love. She asked him about the scar on his thigh and when he told her about being shot, she bent down and kissed it. Even though Noah had a thousand questions, they could wait. Later, after they had calmed down, Ann began to tell Noah what had happened to her.

"I know you talked to Rachael and she told you about our life in the camps. When the trucks that were carrying us stopped, I jumped out and began to run. I was almost to the woods when the guards began firing on us. Suddenly, I felt a sharp pain to the side of my head. In my weaken state I stumbled and fell down, losing consciousness. When I came to, I was lying in a field with dead bodies all around me. I didn't remember what had happened or why I was there. It was raining and cold and I was uncertain what I should do. Finally, I started walking down the road until I came to a farmhouse. The family who lived there took me in and were very kind, even though they were German. The bullet had merely grazed my head, but I was in a state of shock. In addition, I was suffering from malnutrition. They tended my wound, gave me clean clothes, fed me, and nursed me back to health.

I know they saw my tattoo and my prison clothes, but they never mentioned either. I learned that they had lost a son and two nephews in the war. Perhaps their kindness was because of their loss, or maybe they knew the war was lost and almost over, or they may even have known what had been going on in the camps and were sympathetic or ashamed. It may have been all of it. In any case they were very kind to me."

She brushed her hand through her hair, showing him the scar on the side of her head and again he noticed the streaks of grey. "I gradually regained my strength, but I still could not remember who I was or how I got there. Oh Noah, they had taken my wedding ring in the camp, so I didn't even know I was married." She cried as he held her. Taking a deep breath, she continued.

"I stayed there for many months, until the end of the war. One day they brought me the medallion that I had sewn into my clothes. I stared at it, turning it over in my hand. I read our names." She let out a sob, and once again Noah took her in his arms, holding her until she was ready to resume.

"I still was not able to put it all together, but I knew it was the key to my past. Finally, word came that the war was over and the husband came to tell us. He had a bottle of champagne he had been saving and he opened it. Darling, when I heard it pop, I suddenly began to remember! It took a while for me to sort it all out, but after

I regained my memory, I knew I had to leave my safe haven and make my way back to you.

It was not easy. I had to endure a lot of hardships and suffering to travel from Germany, through Belgium, back to Paris. I had no money, no identification, and no way to contact you or anyone else. I was one of the great mass of the displaced, trying to start over. When I finally reached home, Rachael was there. Needless to say, she was shocked. When she finally recovered she told me you had come looking for me and that she had told you I was dead. At first, I wanted to let you know immediately, but the more I considered it, I knew I had to make sure you still wanted me. I was afraid you may have remarried; after all, you thought I was dead. Even if you hadn't, I had lost so much weight I looked like a scarecrow. I had dark circles under my eyes and stringy hair and I didn't want you to see me like that. Noah, I'm so sorry that I didn't let you know immediately, but I was not thinking straight. I was exhausted and needed to rest and regain my strength. Soon I realized I could wait no longer and I contacted my Uncle, swearing him to secrecy. He was very kind and sent me the money for the journey. He also told me where you were. I talked to your parents and they told me it was the miracle they had been praying for and assured me that there was nothing in this world you would want more than for us to be together. I started to call you but decided to surprise you. They promised not to ruin the reunion and added that they hoped you had a strong heart. My darling, I am so proud of you and I love you so very, very much." She began to cry.

"Forever?" he asked through his tears.

"And a day." she answered, smiling, as they held each other once again.

Later they went out to eat and on the way they passed a church. Noah turned to Ann.

"Wait here just a moment; there is something I have to do." He turned and walked into the sanctuary, where he dropped to his knees and, asking forgiveness, thanked God for returning Ann to him. When he came out Ann saw that he was smiling.

"Are you, all right?" She asked.

"Oh yes my love, I couldn't be more right," he replied, taking her into his arms and hugging her tight as he twirled her around on the sidewalk.

CHAPTER 25

The days following Ann's return flew by in a whirl of euphoric bliss. Noah was re-energized with new found enthusiasm to finish his residency. More than once, his fellow students commented to him about how happy he looked. He was no longer referred to as 'The Ghost' and actually began to make friends, even a German medical student. He and Ann entertained some of their newfound friends at home, and even went out occasionally. Ann took a job at a bookstore and insisted that Noah eat regular meals instead of the junk food on which he had been subsisting. When they finally collapsed into bed each night they were exhausted, but always found time to hold each other, occasionally making love and before falling asleep would tell each other, "I love you". It became their mantra and each would repeat it the next morning when they awoke. They never let a day or night go by without expressing their love for each other.

One night, as they lay in each other's arms, Ann looked at Noah and said, "You know sweetheart, in a way I'm glad we went through what we did".

Noah looked at her incredulously. "What do you mean?" He asked.

"When we met that summer, we were so young and filled with a passion for the moment. Neither of us had any real idea about what we wanted out of our lives or future. In a way we were trying to maintain the dream world we were living in." She said.

"I knew I wanted to return to Fairview with you and remain there forever. But in reality, I didn't have any idea how to achieve it. We were just kids," he said, giving her a kiss. "I only knew I didn't want to face a future without you. I guess we've both grown up."

"Umm, I know. Me too, but we really didn't know how to handle everything else. I know I had all kinds of thoughts and fears. I could only see us in that moment in time. For me it was a kind of safety net. Those moments were something to hold on to and allow thoughts about tomorrow to be held at bay. I think it has taken all that has happened to make me realize how precious real love is and that if you have it, nothing else matters. Everything else may come and go, but mature love like ours that's been forged in the fires of adversity will overcome anything that life throws at it." Ann said.

She reached down, took his arm that was around her and placed his hand over her heart. "I love you now even more than I did then, and I know that it will continue to grow, until I burst or die. And even after." She said.

Noah pulled her tighter to him and said, "I don't deserve this much happiness. You know, I think that no matter how little money we have and how hectic things are, someday we'll look back on these days as some of the most satisfying we ever have known. Then to himself he said, "Thank you God."

Graduation day arrived and Noah's parents, along with Michael, attended. Noah was sorry his grandparents could not be there due to their health concerns. After the ceremony, his parents, along with Ann, who had sat with them, came over to where he was standing.

"We are really proud of you, son," his father said, as he shook Noah's hand. "Your grandparents, Sam and Thelma send all their love."

"Congratulations," Michael said, reaching out to shake his hand.

"Thanks." Noah responded, seeing for the first time that his little brother had grown into a poised young man. He was even wearing a suit and tie. Noah was so glad that he had missed the war.

"We love you, Noah," his mother said, as she hugged and kissed him. Noah noticed that her hair was now its original brunette color. Then she moved to Ann and put her arm around her.

"I am so very sorry for the way I treated you when we first met. I admit I had different dreams for Noah, but they were my dreams, not his. I now realize you are part of Noah and a special part of our family. My dear, I hope you will forgive me." She looked apprehensively at Ann, who nodded her consent and then embraced her.

Noah looked away for a minute, not wanting to expose his tears.

The next few weeks were a blur of activity. They moved back with Noah's parents so they could make arrangements for the move to Fairview. Awhile later a letter arrived from his grandparents.

Noah,

Words are inadequate to tell you how proud your Grandmother and I are of you. How grateful we are to God that you and Ann found each other again and will soon be back here to stay. I have prayed for this day since I watched you pull your first trout out of the lake. Beyond your youthful enthusiasm, I could see how inquisitive and passionate you were, both are qualities that will make you a great physician. I don't know how or why, but I realized then that you were meant to be here.

Now that Ann is with you, the circle is complete. There is a reason for everything, even if we do not always know what it is and I think God has given you both that insight.

Everyone is anxiously waiting for your return. Thelma said you can babysit Sam Junior anytime. He is walking and quite a handful, but she says that is the "Sam" in him.

Noah, we want you and Ann to live here at the cabin with us. We can add a room, if needed, and you will be close to the clinic. After all, one day soon it will all be yours.

God bless you both.

Love,

Granddad

The day of departure had finally arrived, and for the first time, Noah had mixed feelings about leaving his family. Ann and his mother were behaving like they were long-lost relatives. His mother had dragged out all the old photograph albums and they spent hours going over them, reliving old memories. They even found time to plan for Noah and Ann's remarriage, once they returned to Fairview. Louise and Ruth had taught Ann about cooking and Noah had even taught her how to drive. These were halcyon days, heightened with joy over the newfound love between his wife and his mother.

The old '37 Chevrolet he had received as a birthday present was packed and they were ready to leave. Noah felt a little apprehensive about the journey since Ann had awakened with an upset stomach and no appetite.

"Maybe we should wait another day to leave," Noah said.

"Don't be silly. I'll be all right. Probably something I ate last night that didn't agree with me. I already feel better." Ann said.

"You be careful," his father said, shaking Noah's hand.

"Good luck," Michael responded.

His mother hugged him and then gave Ann a hug and said, "I'm going to miss you." His mother called out as they drove away, "Call when you get there. We love you both."

Noah could not help marveling over the change in his mother's attitude. As he looked back, he noticed that she and his father were holding hands.

The trip was uneventful. Ann was soon feeling better so Noah let her drive for a while on some of the more deserted parts of the road. They talked about his grandfather's offer to share the house and decided it made sense, at least for now. "I can help Mary around the house. Besides, I really could use some more pointers on cooking, I'd hate to poison you," Ann said with a laugh. "You could keep a watch on George."

"I love you," he said.

"Forever?" She questioned, as she kept her eyes on the road ahead.

"And a day," he replied, with a smile.

CHAPTER 26

They arrived late in the day, and most of the town was there to meet them. Noah and Ann hugged George and Mary, they had told them of their decision to live with them. Noah could see how it pleased them. The Zimmerman's also greeted them with enthusiasm.

"Good to see you both. We have been praying for this day." Ira said shacking Noah's hand. "I'm looking forward to filling those prescriptions for you, Doc."

"Thanks for all your help," Noah told him.

Ann hugged her aunt and uncle, then George and Mary. They spent several minutes, alternately laughing and crying. Suddenly there was barking and Beau came running up.

"Hey fellow, good to see you." Noah said leaning down to scratch Beau's head.

Noah felt a hand on his shoulder. "Welcome back." Noah turned and saw Sam and Thelma. She was holding the hand of a small boy.

"Noah, this is Sam Junior," Thelma said.

Noah gave her a kiss, then reached down and picked him up.

"Hey there, Sam Junior, you sure are lucky. You've got your mother's looks." Feeling a tear well up, he thought, "I'm lucky too. Thank you God."

Ann hugged both Thelma and Sam.

"Let me hold him," Ann said, taking Sam Junior.

"You're going to have to get busy and have one of your own," Thelma said to her. Ann began to blush and Thelma laughed as she turned to Noah. "You hear me," she said, pointing her finger at him.

"Yes ma'am, I'll see what I can do," he replied with a wink and a laugh.

They visited a little longer, until George spoke up, addressing the crowd.

"Noah and Ann have had a long day, and I know they are tired. Mary and I are going to help them unpack, and after we enjoy these wonderful dishes you were so kind to bring, they can get a good night's rest. My friends, they are here to stay, and will have ample opportunity to visit with all of you." George said.

After everyone said their goodbyes, Sam stayed behind to help Noah unload the car. After a few moments, Noah stopped and turned to Sam.

"Thanks Sam, for everything." Noah said.

"Good to have you back, but there is one thing I want to ask you, though." Sam said.

"What's that?" Noah asked.

"Did you cut down your wedding tree?" Sam asked.

Noah, looking sheepishly, explained how he had come back late one night after returning from the war. Thinking Ann was dead he had cut down the tree and left, not wanting to be seen.

"Well, just like you and Ann, it must have strong roots, because it's growing back." Sam said.

Noah smiled then put his arm around Sam. "Thanks again."

After Noah and Ann unpacked and freshened up, they sat down to a wonderful dinner. George offered up a prayer.

"God, Father of all people, we thank you for bringing Ann and Noah back to us. Watch over them and the people they will serve. Let them live long and happy lives. Grant them wisdom and compassion as they tend to the needs of your people. Bless this food to the nourishment of our bodies and us to your service. Amen."

"Boy, this is some spread," Noah said, rubbing his hands eagerly.

"Yes, and all prepared with love," replied George.

They ate and talked of plans for the future until long after midnight. Not wanting it to end but knowing that tomorrow would come soon, Noah and Ann said their goodnights and headed to their room.

"Ann and I would like to get up early and hike up to the rock outcropping." Noah said.

"That sounds like a great idea. Good night and sleep well," George said.

As they got up from the table, George added, "I'd like us all to go fishing soon. I think old Beau and I can still make it."

"We'd like that very much," Ann said, walking around the table and hugging him. "I'll try not to show you two up."

They fell into bed, worn out by the travel and excitement of the day. Before they went to sleep Ann said, "You know, this does feel like home."

"It does, now that you're here," Noah replied, giving her a kiss.

They awoke as the first light of day shown through the window. "Boy, smell that bacon," Noah said, his voice still thick with sleep.

Ann did not answer and Noah noticed she seemed upset.

"What's wrong? Are you okay?" He asked

"My stomach is upset. I don't know what's wrong. Maybe I should talk to your grandfather." Ann replied.

"Good idea," Noah said, giving her a kiss. "Do you want me to get him?"

"No. You go and eat. I don't think I can eat anything. I'll lie here for a few minutes then get dressed so we can go on our hike." She saw the anxiety in his face and reassured him, "go on, I'll be all right."

His grandmother had a breakfast of eggs, bacon and biscuits on the kitchen table.

"Good morning. Boy that sure smells good." Noah said.

"Good morning dear. Where's Ann?" Mary asked.

"She's not feeling too good. Her stomach is upset again. She's been under the weather for several days. We thought Granddad might have a look at her." Noah said.

"I think I'll go and check on her while you finish your breakfast." Mary said, pouring him more coffee.

She knocked on the door and entered to find Ann sitting on the edge of the bed.

"How are you feeling dear?" Mary asked

"Better," Ann replied.

"How long have you felt this way?" Mary asked.

"About a week," Ann said.

"Mostly in the morning?" Mary asked, smiling sweetly.

"Yes, I seem to get better during the day. Probably just a bug I picked up. I'm sure I'll be fine in a day or two." Ann answered.

"Honey, I think you'll be okay in about seven or eight months," Mary said with a big smile.

Ann looked at her incredulously, and then it dawned on her. "You mean ....?"

"You're pregnant!" Mary said, giving her a hug.

Ann was stunned as the realization sunk in. "You're sure?" She asked.

"Honey, believe me, I know." Mary replied.

They hugged each other again.

"Don't tell Noah. I want to surprise him." Ann said.

When Ann came into the kitchen, Noah noticed she was smiling.

"How are you feeling?" He asked.

"Great," she said, seeming to be a lot more cheerful.

"Good. Do you want something to eat?" He asked.

"Maybe just some toast. Then we can get started." Ann said.

Noah noticed her more upbeat demeanor.

It was a glorious summer morning. The night moisture had collected in the low spots, forming small pools of morning mist that rippled when they walked through them. The meadow between the lake and the mountains was a riot of color from every kind of wildflower, giving the appearance of a million flags, all waving in the gentle morning breeze. They held hands and laughed with a natural exuberance at the sheer joy of being alive and in love.

"God, this is heaven," Noah said, giving Ann a hug.

"It is, now that we're here together," Ann said. "When I was a little girl, my mother would tell me that the wind on my face was made by the beating of angel wings. I remember I would sit upstairs in my bedroom and look out the window and pretend I was a princess and all Paris was my kingdom. Then I came to this place and met my king and I became his queen," she said, tilting her head up, kissing him.

They followed the stream up the mountain until they reached the rock. It was unchanged, standing as a monument to their love and their life together. They both stood mesmerized as they soaked in the scene, reliving all that had transpired at this special place. Noah took Ann into his arms and gave her a long, passionate kiss, then reached into his pocket and handed her a small box. She opened it, and with a gasp of delight saw his grandmother's ring that she was to have received so long ago.

"I've been saving it for the repeating of our wedding vows," he explained.

"Oh Noah, it's beautiful!" She put it on her finger. Holding up her hand to admire the ring she said, "I'll never take it off." She smiled, looking at him through happy tears. 'Noah, make love to me." She asked.

"Now. Here?" He asked.

"Yes, oh yes, my love." She said taking him into her arms.

They had put their clothes on but lay cuddling each other.

"Noah, promise me we will never leave here." She said.

"I promise." He said.

"When I die, I want you to scatter my ashes right here." she said.

"Same for me, but we have a lot of living to do first." he said.

"You're right. You need to get your practice going and we need to think about adding another room." She said.

"Another room? Why do we need to…wait a minute, are you saying…you're not…we're not…?" He sat up and looked at her quizzically.

Ann laughed and shook her head yes.

"How, when?" He asked.

"Some doctor you're going to make. I think you know how and it won't be for another seven or eight months." She said with a laugh.

They embraced, alternately laughing and crying with sheer emotion.

Noah was the first to speak. "I love you so. I can't begin to tell you how much."

"Forever?" Ann asked.

"Oh yes, my love, forever, and for all the days to come," He said taking her into his arms.

PRESENT

Noah was pulled from his reverie by the raucous sound of a crow perched in a tree near him. He realized how tired he had become, feeling every bit of his considerable years. Even though it was cooler now, he was perspiring and he reached up to wipe his brow, noticing as he did that his arm seemed sluggish. He closed his hand around the claw necklace he still wore, feeling an odd sense of comfort.

His gaze returned to the ant and saw that it was now joined by several others. They were all working as a team, some pushing and some pulling, all working together to move the beetle carcass along.

"With a little help from my friends," he said aloud, thinking about how his life had been determined by his family and friends and the incredible love they each had showered on him.

His mind was pulled back to another time, becoming mixed with current reality as the faces of his loved ones danced in his memory. He and Ann had kept their promise and spent their life ministering to their friends in Fairview. They had continued to live in the home of his grandparents. The clinic had been turned into additional living space for their growing family. At a different location a new clinic and a small hospital, named after his grandfather, had been built. For a long time, he had been the only doctor in the growing town and had to maintain increasingly longer hours, yet it had been infinitely satisfying work. He had said goodbye to many old friends but had said hello to many new ones too.

Noah and Ann had two children; a son David, who followed in Noah's footsteps and became a doctor and continued the tradition by taking over his practice at Fairview; and a daughter, Rachael, after Ann's sister. Both were now married and live in Fairview, blessing him with five grandchildren and two great-grandchildren. He and Ann had repeated their vows before both a minister and a rabbi. This time his parents were there, and Michael gladly wore a suit. Their religious differences had been worked out. Ann retained her Jewish heritage and faith, although she would accompany Noah and their children to church. They would celebrate Passover and she instructed Noah in holding the Sader meal. There was always a

Christmas and a Hanukah celebration. It may not have been theologically correct but it worked for them. Plus, David and Rachel loved the two holidays. Ann, with the help of Thelma and Mary, had become quite a good cook and had with the help of her aunt even learned how to prepare matzah ball soup, blintzes and knishes. Her chicken soup had become legendary; Noah would refer to it as "Jewish penicillin." Both he and the children, however, had drawn the line on her attempt at gefilte fish, preferring to eat their fish fried. Ann took up the piano again, and for many years the sound of music and laughter could be heard coming from the cabin. They experienced their first winter in the mountains and loved it; their entire family becoming avid skiers.

Recently, a ski resort had been built and that had brought more development to the valley. Noah and Ann had led the effort to have their mountain declared a wilderness area so it would remain preserved and protected as they had always known it.

They made a trip back to Paris for their twentieth wedding anniversary but Ann surprised him when, after only a week, she said that she missed home and was ready to leave. Before leaving, they traveled to Germany to visit the family that had taken care of Ann. They found the house only to discover that, in a twist of fate, the family had immigrated to America shortly after the war. They had tried to locate them but were never successful.

Noah missed his grandfather, even today, and his folksy wisdom and advice. His absence left a huge hole in his heart. Fishing had never seemed the same after his Grandfather's death, even though Noah had learned to tie flies and taught his children and grandchildren how to fish. He thought of his grandmother, with her quiet gentleness. He pictured his mother and father, who only years later realized that in their own way they loved each other. His mother and Ann had learned to love each other over the years and she had become a doting grandmother, but even more amazing, she had become close to Thelma and Sam. He remembered David, still feeling the loss, missing his friendship after all these years. They had named their son after him.

The Zimmerman's sold their store and moved to Florida where they both had relatives, leaving Beau behind to stay until his death with Noah's family. He and Ann had visited them on several occasions and both the children loved going to the beach.

Ted had indeed become a minister in the Methodist church and, after retiring, had returned to Fairview with his wife. He thought of Michael, who had fought in Korea, sustaining an injury that left him with a permanent limp. But at least he had come back home, had married, had three children, and took over their father's grocery store operation. Over the years, he created a large chain that today was one of the more successful operations in the country. Noah and Ann had become godparents to Michael's and Jane's three children, considering them almost their own.

Sam and Thelma had lived a good life, their happiness marred only by the death of their son, Sam Junior, in Vietnam. It had been devastating, but he had left behind a wife and two children who came to live with them. Their presence gave them solace and a reason to carry on.

Noah remembered the wedding tree he had cut down and how it had come back from its roots. "Like life," he thought, "if the roots are strong, it will weather everything that happens, even death." There was now a grove of wedding trees and counting all the grandchildren there would be many more to come. He pictured a forest of trees spreading as far as he could see.

Rachael and her husband had immigrated to Israel, adopted two Jewish refugee children, and lived there until their deaths many years later. The two families had visited each other many times over the years.

He reached in his pocket and took out an envelope that contained the last letter Ann had written to him. She wrote it as her health began to fail. He took it out of its protective envelope and holding it in his trembling hands began to read.

My Darling,

As I write this I have wonderful thoughts and memories of you that flow gently across my mind like soft summer breezes.

You have always been there: never far from my heart. I rummage through boxes of old photographs like a prospector seeking treasure beyond price. Suddenly there you are and I want to shout "Eureka", but a tear gets in the way. How young we were and how much in love. I do not cry for that rather I revel in it, wrapping it around me with an understanding that life is a hostage to time and timing. I wrote the following poem giving voice to my emotions.

IS It Real

Is this real or only an illusion, I ask Myself;
Surely, I am not entitled to this much happiness.

Yet when I hold you, or kiss you, or just talk to you,
The answer comes with incredible clarity.
It is real and maybe everything else is illusion.
My love for you is the one certainty in a world
Full of ambiguity;
And if this earthly orb we occupy should disappear,
My love would continue through empty time
And space, forever and a day.
Your loving wife,
Ann

He placed the letter back in the envelope and returned it to his pocket. He wiped a tear from his eye and then settled back against the rock face as he thought how all of his generation was gone now, even his beloved Ann, who had died five years ago. They had both decided on cremation and following those wishes, her ashes had been scattered at this very spot, as his would be. Noah could still remember some of the last words she said to him as he sat holding her hand.

"You know dearest, it's not death I fear, it's the absence of you."

He knew he would soon join her and all the others, but he had no fear, only a sense of relief.

How quickly it had all gone by. It seemed like only yesterday when he had looked up from this very spot and saw a dog, followed by a girl in a yellow sundress. He wondered why he was the only one left and then he remembered when he was very small and had thrown a handful of pebbles into a pond and watched as each one created an ever-expanding circle in the water, each circle overlapping another. "Maybe", he thought, "that's what it's all about. Each one of us makes a ripple in the fabric of our life and each ripple combines with others until they become one unending swell that goes on forever." He laughed to himself, "Granddad would be proud of me."

As he closed his eyes, his head, along with his shoulder, began to hurt with a sharper pain and he leaned back against the granite rock, relishing the coolness of its surface. Slowly he began to feel himself sinking, becoming one with the rock, the grass, the earth, the universe.

He awoke with a start, marveling at how refreshed he felt. He was considering this when a movement caught his eye. He looked up and saw in the woods, at the transition between light and shadow, a black dog that looked familiar. Suddenly, a figure appeared, and as he squinted to better focus, he saw a young girl in a yellow sundress, her black hair cascading around her shoulders. She smiled and held out her hand for him to join her. Noah got up and was astonished to realize he felt completely renewed. He moved with a spring in his step to where the dappled light played over her. She was as beautiful as ever and he felt joy and exhilaration at seeing the medallion around her neck. He bent down and stroked the dog's back, then straightened, as he reached out and took her hand. She began to lead him into the shadows, but before they entered, he turned and looked back at the rock. Sitting on the ground with his head leaning against the hard surface was an old man. Noah studied him for a moment, finding it curious that the old man was smiling. Then he turned back and the three of them walked into the woods.

THE END

Made in the USA
Lexington, KY
04 May 2018